Heart of the Witch

by

Debbie Peterson

This is a work of fiction. Names, characters, places, and incidents are either the product of the author's imagination or are used fictitiously, and any resemblance to actual persons living or dead, business establishments, events, or locales, is entirely coincidental.

Heart of the Witch

Cover Art by *Debbie Taylor*

The Wild Rose Press, Inc.
PO Box 708
Adams Basin, NY 14410-0708
Visit us at www.thewildrosepress.com

Publishing History
First Fantasy Rose Edition, 2020
Trade Paperback ISBN 978-1-5092-3128-7
Digital ISBN 978-1-5092-3129-4

Published in the United States of America

Dedication

To Rhonda Penders and RJ Morris—
my heartfelt gratitude for planting me
in your rose garden where I could grow and flourish.
Thank you, Lisa Dawn,
for all you have done and do for me personally.
To Debbie Taylor,
who has created such beautiful covers for me,
I thank you.
And a special thank you to my two wonderful editors,
Sarah and Claudia.
You've both taught me so much over the years,
and I appreciate your patience and dedication in
working with me.
~
And David, as always, you have my heart.

Chapter One

San Juan, Puerto Rico
September 1628

"We've got her! Tell Manera we've got his witch!"

"Are you sure it's her?" a voice, more distant than the first, called out.

"Of course, it's her, you jolthead," he replied. "Who else would she be? Now, go find out where your beetle-headed taskmaster wants her put."

"Can't you see I'm a little busy right now, Gilbert? See to it yourself," said the second man.

"Tell your trollop goodnight and do as you're told!" a third man growled.

"Oh, come on Arthur," he whined. "I can't get to the fortress any faster than you can, now can I?"

The back and forth exchange between the three men drifted into her mind like a slow-moving avalanche. She blinked away the mist that clouded her thoughts.

"You know we don't speak your language, Lico," Gilbert said. "And we don't fancy holding onto Manera's prize any longer than necessary, being she is who you say she is. Still, the man won't be pleased if we turn her loose, eh?"

Wait! Are they...are they talking about me?

Full awareness now enveloped her. Lissabeth

Capoen lowered her gaze as she slyly peeked toward one side then the other. Her heart doubled its pace as she gazed at the brown boots to her left and the black boots to her right.

Two men held her fast. Another was somewhere behind her. Instinct overrode rational thought as she struggled for freedom. In response, her captors viciously tightened their grip on her arms. Pain shot from her forearms to her shoulders. Despite the agony, her nails dug into her palm as she clung to the crystal in her hand. All the while she prayed they wouldn't see it.

"Let's go, wench," Arthur snarled. "And no tricks or you'll soon wish you hadn't, hear me? Should I fancy it, I could break a woman like you in pieces."

Lissabeth didn't say a word as they dragged her out of the forest. They passed through the gates that led to the citadel. The heavy wooden doors at the top of the steps creaked opened. Armando Manera stepped out into the night with a torch in his hand. The ugly, scar-faced, hefty little man gazed into her eyes and grinned. His smile grew ever broader as her captors forced her up the stairs toward him.

"This way." Armando beckoned her guards with a wave of his hand. He led them down a darkened stone hallway and into an even darker room off to the right. The men thrust her to the floor where she landed face down. She propped herself up on her elbows as she turned slightly to her side. With her cloak providing cover, she quickly stuffed her crystal deep inside her bodice.

"Get up," Armando commanded.

Someone yanked her to her feet while another lit the torches in the empty, windowless room.

"Now," said Armando. "Take off her cloak and shake it out."

Lissabeth didn't move as the guards jumped to his bidding. All the while she gazed into Manera's eyes.

Armando extended his hand toward her skirt. "Remove those pouches at her sides and hand them to me."

Once he had them both in his possession, Manera undid the ties of the smallest bag and turned it upside down. Her precious herbs spilled onto the stone floor. Armando kicked at the pile, scattering seeds, roots, stems and blossoms in all directions. He methodically gazed over every inch of the flooring. All throughout his search, his knitted brows drew ever closer together. With his lips stretched tight, he ripped the second pouch open. He stuffed his hand inside the bag and tore out the clothing she had brought with her. His search through the fabric yielded nothing. He scooped up her cloak, wadded it up along with her dresses, and tucked the lot underneath his arm.

"Where is your vile charm, *Señorita* Capoen?"

"I dropped it in the forest," she ground out. "If you want it, you'll have to send your drudges out to find it."

His small, beady eyes narrowed. "Your haughtiness is ill-suited under your present circumstances, *sí*?"

Lissabeth said nothing.

Armando strode toward the door and grasped the latch. He then turned toward the guards. "Clear the room of all the debris from her pouch. I don't want a single speck of dust left behind. Once you've completed the task, provide our prisoner just the barest of necessities. That includes both food and water."

No one spoke or even glanced in her direction as the men swept the room. Along with some straw, they brought in a filthy, tattered mattress and dropped it onto the floor. They left her with a single torch, then shut and locked the door.

Days passed, five of them, *if* they fed her once a day as they said they would. In all those days she had but one vision. One. Yet, it was enough. That vision told her that her sister was alive and still inside the citadel—

The door swung open with a stuttered moan. Several men followed Armando inside.

"Get her to her feet and be quick about it! Make sure she doesn't escape, or you'll personally answer to the *padre*."

One of the men placed a blindfold over her eyes while another shackled her wrists. Then they led her out of the fortress in chains. She took in a deep breath of fresh air as the warmth of the sun caressed her face. But where were they taking her? The sound of the ocean waves grew louder with each step she took.

Dear heaven, are they taking me to a ship? What about my sister? Lissabeth listened for any small noise that would tell her she had accompanied them on their trek.

"Margaretha, are you here?" she called. Silence answered the question.

A swirling mist invaded her mind while a warm flush spread through her veins. No! She mustn't have a vision right now! Not with Manera watching!

Within her mind's eye, ships burst into vivid view. Allegiance separated them as they faced off, one side against the other. A single bellowed command echoed in the distance. The deafening roar of cannon fire followed. Thunderous booms muffled the shouted orders of the officers in charge. The overwhelming smell of gunpowder followed bright flashes of fire and smoke. Through the haze the flags of the Spanish fleet billowed in the breeze. So did the banners that belonged to the Dutch West India Company. The ship upon which she sailed headed straight toward the fray.

"Kapitein! Ship off the starboard bow!"

Her gaze shifted toward the man who spoke. He lowered his spy-glass and hollered out the warning. She glanced at the broad-shouldered captain who stood near the railing his back facing her. He wore a loose-fitting white shirt. His jerkin, breeches and knee-high boots were black, while his leather belt was dark umber. His dark brown, shoulder-length hair flowed freely in the breeze.

In response to the threat, the captain turned his gaze right in search of the enemy vessel. He moved a half-step forward and lifted a hand.

"Man the guns, Johannes! Come alongside and fire at wi—"

She gasped as a ball from a musket slammed into his heart. He collapsed onto the deck just as a blast from a cannon ball whizzed through the air. The projectile blew a gaping hole in the side of his ship. The vessel convulsed against the violent impact. Water rushed in through the breach. The ship listed dangerously to port. Despite the struggle she found her footing as best she could and bolted toward the captain. Her hands covered her mouth as she dropped to his side. She fixed her gaze solely on his wound. Several pairs of legs gathered around their commander. No one uttered a single word. She spared them nary a glance. Instead, she stared at the blood that soaked his shirt. Too much blood.

Oh no. No, no, no.

Out of desperation she placed her hand over his chest and pressed down as hard as she could on the horrific gash—

****

Lissabeth gasped as the vision abruptly ended. Salty water trickled down her face and into her mouth. She wiped it away as best she could with shackled hands. Someone held her in his arms. He removed her blindfold and flung it as she coughed up the brine. Another man, with an empty bucket in his hand, stared at her.

"Is she all right?" one of the soldiers asked.

"I think she fainted," said the man who held her.

"Wouldn't surprise me with what little food they've given her," muttered the first.

"She's fine, I tell you. Get her to her feet and into the ship," Armando commanded. "Hurry! *Capitán* Galardi wants to set sail immediately."

As they led her toward the galleon, the awful vision replayed in her mind, a vision in which she was a participant. How did she get there? When would the event come to pass? Who were those people on board that ship?

She didn't think on it overly long. Minutes later, Lissabeth stood in front of a dark little room below deck. Sullied straw, a woolen blanket and a small lantern served as its only furnishings. In addition, strange markings were carved on the door. She strained to see what they looked like—

Armando thrust her inside the foul prison berth. His sneer gave way to an evil, menacing grin as he chained her wrist to the beam. He gave the chain a tug.

"As you can see, we've made escape impossible. At the same time, we've rendered you powerless through a blessed power far greater than the evil one you hold so dear. Therefore, you would do well to do as you're told. Should you think otherwise, you, as well as your sister, will suffer the consequences of your willful actions. This is something you wouldn't want on your conscience, would you?"

Lissabeth said nothing in return. She didn't utter a word of protest when Manera's men closed the door, locked it and then nailed it shut.

Days passed without her seeing a soul. Through her visions, she now knew with certainty her sister was not onboard this ship. The only contact she had with any member of the crew was when someone slid a bowl of food underneath the door.

Lissabeth eased herself back onto the straw after another meager meal. Her gaze traveled the length of the wall from the floor up toward the deck-head and back again. The echo of creaking wood produced the only music in her otherwise silent prison. She welcomed the sound.

The sudden chill that invaded the berth meant the sun had set once again. She wrapped the tattered woolen blanket snugly around her shoulders as best she could. Overhead, the small lantern swayed with the gentle rolling motion of the ship. She watched for a time as the dim light cast eerie shadows on the walls, shadows that conjured faces and full-bodied apparitions if she watched them long enough.

A sudden uproar overhead ended her thoughts. For several minutes, a clamor of footsteps, thuds, thumps and shouts reverberated throughout the galleon. So did the unmistakable sound of steel as it clashed against steel. Seconds turned to minutes as an intense fight raged above her. At last, all grew quiet. Muffled voices broke through the stillness. She couldn't understand a single word they said from where she sat.

Ruthless pirates sailed these waters. Everyone knew that.

Was it a mutiny or something far worse?

****

"I believe I have you at a disadvantage, *Capitán*. You needn't pretend you don't understand me. It's quite clear you do," said Rand Van Locken.

A snort followed the comment. "A disadvantage, sir? That much is rather obvious. You've a blade at my throat."

"Indeed I do, and it has a razor-sharp edge. The way I see it, you may surrender and live or you can command your men to fight and die. Do keep in mind, sir; you'll be the first to test my claim should dying be the course you choose." He paused. "The choice is yours, of course."

"You'll allow me the dignity of getting dressed first? I don't fancy prancing about in my nightclothes in front of my men," he snapped.

"Nay, I don't think so. By now your men are awaiting orders. We shouldn't keep them waiting any longer, should we? They are quite frightened to say the least."

The Spaniard glared but said nothing as he rose from his bed. Rand forced him up the rungs to the upper

8

deck. The galleon's captured crewmen stood guarded by the well-seasoned men of the *Rood Draeck*. He hadn't removed the threat of his sword from the captain's throat.

The tardy Spaniards who scrambled up the side ladders with weapons drawn, halted in their tracks. Their gazes darted between their captain and the wicked-looking cutlass that threatened his life. Dread and uncertainty set in. The slackness of their jaws, their widened eyes, and the slow heave of their chests was proof of that.

Good. Perhaps they needn't spill any more blood tonight.

The captain of the galleon took in a shallow breath and gulped several times over. "Lay down your weapons men. Do as you're told, and your lives will be spared."

The clamor of abandoned weapons followed the order. Rand's crewmen secured all prisoners and tossed all enemy weapons into the boats below. Then at his order they conducted their captives down to the hold and locked them inside. As his men returned, they reported that the place was void of treasure.

Yet, experience told him the lack was naught but a ruse.

"Let's see what hidden valuables this ship has to offer the West India Company, shall we? From all accounts we should find considerable treasure within her hull, more than enough to delight the Spanish king. Inspect each floor and cubbyhole. We'll not leave without it even if we must tear this ship apart, piece by piece."

The men fanned out in search of hidden places that

would conceal jewels, gold, and silver. Rand crossed the length of the vessel. He descended the next flight of steps and turned toward the fore of the ship. Along the way he searched every niche and compartment he spied. He found lead sheets, repair wood, ballast, gun powder and a few broken crates.

In a matter of minutes, exuberant shouts from the floor above alerted him to the crew's success. Then his gaze fell upon a door. The rough-hewn surface had square crosses, backward threes, squiggly lines, and bug-eyed creatures carved into the wood. An assortment of dried roots and branches with wilted foliage was tacked to the frame in a haphazard manner. The mess had a musty scent that stunk. Odd. Someone had nailed the door shut. Did the Spaniards not think the heavy lock was sufficient?

What the devil?

An empty bowl, save a few rat droppings, lay just outside and to the right of the hastily constructed door. The Spaniard captain or someone in authority had imprisoned someone inside the room—but whom? Why the need for the nails, rotting plant matter, and bizarre symbols? He stepped back and took in a deep breath.

"Laurens?"

His ship's carpenter clambered down the steps. He yanked the pistol out of his belt as his gaze darted about.

"Is there trouble, *Kapitein*?"

"I want this door removed right now."

Laurens studied the lock and rusty hinges on the door. "I'll be right back."

In no time at all Laurens returned with some pilfered tools. He removed the nails and then made quick work of the lock, hinges and latch. The heavy door teetered with the sway of the ship and clattered backward. Rand stood back as he tracked its descent. The timber hit the decking with a couple of resounding thuds.

Rand brushed past Laurens. He entered the dimly lit room with his wheel lock pistol cocked. Instead of a deranged or dangerous blackguard who'd fight tooth and nail for his freedom, his gaze landed on a woman. She had the most exquisite willow-green eyes he'd ever seen. Golden, waist-length curls framed her lovely face.

A thousand different thoughts stormed his mind. Her dirty, tattered, blue-and-white peasant garb didn't note her as anyone of great importance. Therefore, ransom seemed an unlikely reason for her foul imprisonment. Regardless of reason, he didn't find it any wonder the captain had locked her away. Such a woman would tempt any man away from his duty as well as his honor—*if* he allowed it. Yet, if the captain simply wanted his men kept at arm's length, he would've given her his cabin, wouldn't he? And every luxury he could provide as well. He would *not* have locked her inside this dank, filthy hole.

Nonetheless, the boorish captain's motivation for his irrational behavior shouldn't concern him. He couldn't involve himself in her troubles right now. Without question, the moment the prize crew handed the galleon over to Heyn, he would place the girl under the commander's protection. The admiral would care for her in whatever manner he deemed best. In the meantime, he'd settle her inside the Spanish captain's cabin. She could rest there in far greater comfort for the duration of the voyage.

Pleased with his plan, he dipped his head. He took a half step toward her, extended his hand and hoped it put her at ease.

"Good evening, my lady, my name is Rand Van Locken, captain of the *Rood Draeck*. We've just taken possession of this ship on behalf of the Dutch West India Company. You needn't fear me or any member of my crew. I give you my word, we won't hurt you. If you'll allow me the honor, I'll take you to the captain's cabin. The former captain of this ship no longer has a use for it."

For a moment it seemed she considered his words. Her gaze never once left his. It appeared those lovely eyes of hers assessed every portion of his heart, his soul, and even delved into his thoughts. Did she, in some way, find him lacking?

"And come the dawn?" she whispered in her native tongue.

Rand shrugged away her concern as he tucked away both his surprise and curiosity. *How on earth did a Dutch woman fall into the hands of the Spaniards?* He cleared his throat as he shook away the troubling question.

"By then we'll have met up with the main fleet. Admiral Heyn will take charge of this vessel. I'm sure that he or a trusted member of his crew will take you ashore at the first opportunity that presents itself. You needn't worry over any of that right now nor in the days to come. I promise he won't abandon you or leave you defenseless. Heyn is an honorable man. He'll see to your safety as well as your welfare."

The woman slowly rose from her crude bed. She eased the threadbare blanket off her shoulder. As it slid down the length of her arm and onto the floor, his gaze fell on the iron shackle around her bruised and swollen wrist. The heavy chain tethered her to the beam and allowed for very little movement. Rage overshadowed his compassion though he kept his fury in check for her sake.

His quick-tempered carpenter spewed a string of curses. Each threatened the black heart and appendages of all those responsible for her brutal imprisonment.

"After all this madness, they chained her like an animal as well?" Laurens thundered. "Where did they expect she'd go?"

"Find the key, Laurens," Rand said between clenched teeth. "*Now.*"

"I'm on it, *Kapitein*! One way or another, I'll find it."

Indeed he would. Nothing would stop Laurens from completing the given command.

Assuming, of course, the key was on this ship…

Chapter Two

A number of possibilities as well as their consequences filled her mind. Lissabeth gazed back and forth between the two Dutch sailors who had forced their way through the door. As the man called Laurens turned away, he took one last look inside her prison. She didn't miss the wrath in his eyes. One could almost pity the Spaniards who'd feel the outlet for his rage.

Almost.

The attractive, powerfully built captain stepped toward her and took her hand in his. He was dressed in black from head to toe. His thigh-length coat, with gold buttons and trimming, was buttoned to the neck. He had a chestnut-colored beard and mustache that was well trimmed.

This man doesn't look like a pirate.

He busied himself with examining her wrist from every angle. By the knit of his brow, she could see he had plenty of questions.

Finally, he let go of her hand. She met his mesmerizing, indigo-colored gaze once more. It was filled with a mixture of anger and concern.

"You look malnourished. Did they give you anything to eat or drink while you've been a *guest* onboard this ship?"

She glanced at the bowl that now lay half-hidden underneath the fallen door. "They make sure I don't starve," she said slipping into English.

"What's your name?"

"Lissabeth."

Rand Van Locken raked his fingers through the stray locks of his dark brown, shoulder-length hair as he narrowed his eyes. "Tell me, Lissabeth, did anyone on this ship force you to—uh—what I mean to say is, did anyone onboard this ship *hurt* you in any way?"

She understood the underlying meaning of his question and shook her head. Before she could tell him she'd rather have suffered death than endure the vile touch of any man aboard this galleon, Laurens returned with a ring of keys in his hand. In addition, he had Armando Manera, flanked by two of Van Locken's men.

Armando gasped as they approached the open doorway. The Spaniard lifted his fettered hands to his mouth as his eyes grew ever wider.

"No, you mustn't let *her* out. You... you don't know what she's capable of. The woman... she's... she's a witch," he sputtered. "An evil, vile witch."

The captain huffed out a breath as he rolled his eyes heavenward. "Is this the beslubbering codpiece that locked her up, Laurens?"

"Aye, *Kapitein*," said Laurens. "His gutless companions identified him as the architect of this foul, disgusting berth. Manera is his name. Armando Manera. The man is a pig."

Rand heaved out a sigh and snatched the keys from Laurens's hand. Did the Spaniard see the scowl on his face and the fire raging in his eyes as she did? Better yet, did he fear it?

"If you truly believe she's a witch, why would you

take her onboard this ship? On second thought, I've a better question. Where were you planning to take her, and what did you intend to do with her once you arrived at your destination, hmm?"

Armando looked like a mouse in the jaws of a cat. Lissabeth received a small measure of satisfaction when he squirmed like one. Manera spared her a furtive glance but said nothing. That didn't surprise her. He couldn't stand up to a man such as Rand Van Locken. He didn't have the guts. The coward only bullied those far weaker than he.

"I asked you a question. Don't make me ask it again," Rand ground out.

Beads of sweat popped out on Manera's forehead as he gazed up at the man that dwarfed him in both height and size. "Benavides, he…" The man sucked in a breath and stopped short.

Rand gave him a sideways glance. "Yes? Benavides?"

Armando clamped down on his teeth. He cast his gaze to the floor, and squeezed his eyes shut. Dewy liquid formed at the corners of his eyes then drizzled down his cheeks.

"Looks like he's lost his tongue as well as his wits, *Kapitein*. Perhaps the *witch* cast a spell upon him, after all." Laurens spat.

"So be it."

Rand thumbed through the keys for the one that would unlatch the lock. Then released her from her chains. He handed Laurens the shackle and then led her past the fallen door. His scornful gaze fell upon Manera.

"Lock him up. Tight. Remove that pitiful excuse

for a lantern. He doesn't deserve even the smallest portion of its light. Replace the door exactly as you found it. Nail it shut. Add a few boards for good measure if you can find some. But first, put a gag in that reprehensible mouth of his. Should someone find and release him before he starves to death, he can count himself most fortunate."

"No, please," Armando begged as Laurens pushed him inside the compartment. "You must understand; I did only what was necessary to safeguard this ship. The woman—she has a terrible power bestowed upon her by an evil host of demonic beings. Perhaps even the devil himself. I've witnessed it. Don't let her beauty fool you! You'll be sorry if you do and—"

"Shut your mouth and keep it closed."

Armando's shoulders wilted as tears filled his eyes. His lips quivered.

"Please, don't imprison me in here. The place is filled with wickedness. Can't you feel its unholy darkness? Allow me to join my companions in the hold. I'll go willingly. I—"

"Not. Another. Word. Do you understand?" Rand turned and faced her. "Now if you're ready, Lissabeth, I'll take you up to the captain's cabin."

Laurens squeezed the shackle around Manera's wrist. He relentlessly applied pressure well after the Spaniard yelped in pain from the shackle's iron grip. Only then did he turn and face the captain. "Uh, *Kapitein*? May I have a word with you before you leave?"

"You can speak your mind, Laurens," Rand replied. "I've never denied you that."

"Well, it's just that under the current

17

circumstances, I don't think we should leave the girl aboard this vessel. We've not worked with this prize crew before and know nothing of their skills. With all due respect, I know Heyn holds them in the highest regard. He wouldn't have assigned them to the *Draeck* otherwise. Still, something could go awry. If that happens, this girl will be the first to suffer the wrath of every Spaniard aboard this ship. Especially if they believe witchcraft aided their capture."

"Superstitious louts." Rand scraped a hand over his beard as he blew out a sigh. "You're right, of course. She'll sail with us then."

Armando gasped, stamped his foot, and shook his head like a petulant child. "No, no! It's best you leave her aboard the galleon, *Capitán*. You... you would... risk both your ship and the... the lives of your crew if you take her from this ship. She'll bewitch you all and then she'll..."

Rand's eyes filled with renewed contempt as he turned his back on Manera. Laurens jerked a filthy rag from out of his pocket and spat on it. He stuffed it in the man's mouth and then thrust him back against the straw. Manera landed with a loud *oomph*. Pain marred his features.

The captain paid no heed as he gently grasped her hand. He led her up the steps and over to the ladder at the side of the ship. After her descent, a member of his crew settled her into the bobbing boat. The brine of the sea assailed her nose as she took her first deep breath of fresh air since boarding the galleon. She gazed at the large, two-masted ship off to her left. The painted red dragon at the bow of the ship looked fierce. The *Rood Draeck*, indeed.

Rand dipped his head as she met his gaze. "Before we return to my ship, there are a few things that need my attention aboard the galleon. You'll be safe where you are until I return. I give you my word. Is that satisfactory?"

Safe? For the moment, yes. But this brief respite from danger wouldn't last. Somewhere in the immediate future, if not already, Juan Benavides would lose the entire fleet of ships that belonged to the Spanish crown. Along with those ships he'd lose the massive treasure he had collected. In turn, he would earn the wrath of his king. Her recent visions left no doubt of that. Yet, like all her visions, the things she didn't see haunted her thoughts far more than what she saw. She still had questions without answers and that worried her. Despite her uncertainty, she managed a small smile and a grateful nod. "Yes, thank you, *Kapitein* Van Locken. I'm in your debt."

"Not at all, my lady. I'll find it a pleasure to look after you."

In less than an hour, a man named Hendrick Van Meter rowed the boat alongside the *Rood Draeck*. A rope ladder tumbled down from the rail and slapped against the side of the ship. The crewman with the darkest hair and eyes, whom the captain introduced as Joris Hoochlandt, stood up. He took her hand and led her to the ladder. The man Joris called Cornelius held it steady as she climbed. Rand followed a step behind. Another attractive man lifted her up and over the rail. The blue-eyed, sandy-haired man, every bit as tall and impressively built as Rand Van Locken, didn't seem the least bit surprised to see her.

She couldn't say the same.

Surprise, as well as spine-chilling apprehension, clasped icy fingers around her heart the moment her gaze met his.

"Lissabeth, this is my first mate, Wolfaert Dircksen Van Ness. Wolf, this is Lissabeth. We'll see to it that she arrives aboard Admiral Heyn's ship without undue hardship or mishap. Isn't that right?"

"Without question." Wolf gave his captain a casual salute. He then turned his gaze toward her and grinned. "You're a welcome sight aboard the *Draeck*, Lissabeth. It's been quite a while since anyone so lovely graced this ship."

Despite her unease, she returned his welcoming smile as best she could. "Thank you."

Rand put a hand at her elbow and led her in the direction of the stern. Off to the left, they descended a short flight of steps and stopped in front of the door at the bottom. "There's no place more comfortable on this ship than my cabin. Please make use of it in whatever way pleases you best."

"Oh, no. I couldn't, and really, I don't mind—"

"You can, and you will. Captain's orders."

The firm set of his jaw told her she shouldn't argue. "You've been more than kind. Once again, I must thank you."

He invited her inside with a sweep of his hand. As she turned around and faced him, she caught his critical gaze studying every inch of her form. His scrutiny made her quite uncomfortable and self-conscious.

"I'll have our cook bring you something to eat," he said, his rekindled anger evident in tone alone.

"Wait!" She held a hand out as he turned to leave. "Could I have just a minute of your time?"

Without releasing the latch, he nodded. "Certainly."

What to say? "You said earlier you were meeting up with the Dutch fleet?"

"Aye, we expect we'll arrive by dawn. This doesn't trouble you, does it?"

She shook her head. "It's, uh, just simple curiosity as to the direction we're going. I mean, from where you had anchored your ship it looked as if you were sailing in the opposite direction of where we are headed now. That's all."

Rand chuckled. "Naught but a deception began a few days ago. You see, Admiral Heyn ordered half his force to set sail for Europe under the watchful gaze of Benavides and his men. A man whose name you seem familiar with, am I right?"

"Yes, I know who he is." She left it at that.

"Anyway, with half our fleet gone, Heyn knew that Benavides wouldn't feel the least bit threatened by the remaining ships and would finally leave the safety of his port. However, what Benavides doesn't know is that a fair number of those ships are circling back. The Admiral asked that I return my ship this evening as well. He said they could use our help in overtaking the Spanish armada once the fools gathered their courage and ventured out. As you can see, we're a bit overdue. I think we'll have a good enough excuse for the delay, though. Especially once he sees what we have to offer."

Her heart began a slow hammer inside her chest. Still she hoped. "Does that mean that due to the time taken in capturing the galleon, you're too late for the battle?"

"Battle? What battle?"

She sucked in a breath over the mistake. Heat

climbed from her neck to her cheeks.

"Well, you just said that Heyn planned to overtake the Spanish armada and that you were expected earlier. So, I just thought—"

Rand shrugged. "I suppose all things are possible, but are we too late should a battle occur? No, I don't think so. Our tardiness just means we'll have something more to offer Admiral Heyn other than our assistance. A whole lot more. If all goes well, we'll capture the ships without the need for cannon fire or a single shot from a musket. Please, you mustn't worry. We'll keep you safe, I promise."

Her heart dropped into the pit of her stomach as her earlier vision crashed into her mind. Things rarely went according to plan and this time would be no exception. Captain Rand Van Locken calmly sailed toward his death. It was *his* ship she had seen in her vision, even if she had not seen his face, only his gaping wound at the time. On the other hand, Wolfaert Dircksen Van Ness, the captain's first mate? 'Twas he who shouted out the warning just before the musket ball slammed through the captain's heart.

"Now, before you faint dead away, let's get something inside your stomach. Looks to me as if your jailors didn't give you much to eat or drink while they had you in their care."

The door closed before she could respond—before she could warn him of what would happen if they didn't change course. She rushed forward and grasped the latch.

Should I go after him? Would he think I'm crazy if I told him what I saw in vision? Worse yet, would he think I'm the witch Armando accused me of being?

Lissabeth turned around, rested her back against the door, and took in her surroundings. The captain's bed had a thick feather mattress, topped with a blue quilt. A large oak trunk rested at its foot. Its dome-topped coffer was bound in black iron straps. An oak rectangular table with four chairs sat opposite the bed. In between the bed and table was a matching chest with four narrow drawers.

A soft tap on the door interrupted her troubled thoughts.

She bit down on her lip. "Come in."

A stocky gentleman with silver-gray hair and matching beard entered. In one hand, he carried a large plate heaped with smoked beef topped with gravy, carrots and biscuits. In the other, he carried a pewter mug filled with water. She'd never seen such fare on a ship before. Her mouth watered at the aroma and her stomach growled all the louder.

"Well, no wonder the *kapitein* wants you well-fed."

He put the plate and the mug on the small table. With a sweep of his hand, he invited her to sit down. "You're no bigger than a mite. Now, do this ol' cook a favor and eat hearty lest you hurt his feelings beyond repair, hmm? Most folks don't know it, but cooks have sensitive souls, you know."

She met his wink with a small smile. "In that case, I'll do my best to clean my plate."

"The *kapitein* tells me your name is Lissabeth. Mine is Andries Van Halst. If you should find you need anything—anything at all—just ask. Are we agreed on that?"

She could only nod as he bowed at the waist and

then walked out of the cabin.

In deference to the cook, she ate far more than she needed or wanted. When she couldn't force another bite, she headed for the bed. Yet, the comforts of the soft feather mattress escaped her notice, as did the sleep her body craved.

Given Rand's skeptical reaction to Armando's claim, she knew he would dismiss her vision. He'd believe the time spent in her prison affected her mind so much it made her delusional, wouldn't he? No, she couldn't share her vision. She must think of something else. Without knowing it, the captain had provided additional time for the rescue of her sister. Now she must save his life in return. She must find a way before they arrived at their destination where death awaited him and many of his crewmen. After she accomplished that, she'd go after Margaretha.

But what can I possibly do in the time I have left?

The problem worried her for a while. *Ah, but how stupid! I have all the elements I need around me.*

The difficulty would come in the brief amount of time she had left. Could she collect those elements in the quantity she needed? Lissabeth retrieved her faceted, star-shaped, crystal from out of her bodice and placed the delicate, silver chain attached to it around her neck. She focused all her concentration on the ice-blue talisman. Heat now radiated from the crystal and grew warmer as she cradled it in her hands. She closed her eyes, gathering together the water surrounding the ship as well as the layers of both warm and cool air high above the vessel.

As dawn broke, excited voices brought her toward full awareness. Hendrick spotted the Dutch fleet to the starboard side of the ship. He hadn't mentioned the Spaniards. At least, not yet.

"Steady as she goes," said Rand.

"*Kapitein*! Some kind of thick, heavy fog is rolling in westward, and the blasted thing is heading straight toward us," Hendrick bellowed. "I've never seen anything like it in all my days!"

"By all the saints," shouted Joris. "Look at those monstrous clouds, would you? They're about to swallow us whole!"

Indistinguishable voices called out, disbelief and panic within their tone. Rand shouted out commands to keep them from colliding with the Dutch fleet or any other unseen object the deep mist obstructed. For several minutes, footsteps hammered back and forth against the deck in response to those commands.

Had she succeeded then?

She rose from the captain's bed and climbed the steps to the top deck. As she tucked her talisman inside her bodice, the dense fog that had engulfed the ship receded. Little by little, the dark gray clouds rolled away in the face of the strengthening wind. All the crewman on deck faced the sea.

If they searched for Heyn's flotilla she now knew with certainty, they wouldn't find it. The tension that had kept her company since boarding the vessel left her body. She took in a deep breath and let it go.

"Where are all the other ships?" someone asked. "Surely they couldn't have all sunk."

"An entire fleet couldn't possibly sink that fast, you clodpate," chided the fair-haired man named Pieter.

"No, they couldn't," Cornelius replied. "Even if they had, the victors would still be afloat, and we'd see debris scattered on top of the water."

"Where in the blazes are we? That might be the better question right now. The coast is no longer in sight," Joris pointed out. "How is that possible?"

"Give us a position, Wolf," Rand said as he paced back and forth along the deck. He wore the white shirt, jerkin, breeches and knee-high boots she'd seen in her vision.

Wolf took hold of some sort of huge instrument and hefted it onto his shoulder. He fiddled with it for a bit and then put it away. The twinkle in his eyes accompanied his broad smile.

"We're at about twenty-two degrees north, give or take, and heading east with the assistance of what I would deem a rare easterly wind."

Rand stared as he raked his hand through his hair. "That's just not possible."

Wolf wagged his head from side to side and chuckled. "Nay, it isn't. But here we are nonetheless."

Chapter Three

Wolf noticed her the moment she stepped out on the foredeck. He acknowledged her presence with a pleasant smile and a courtly bow. She returned the greeting in like manner. A bit confused over the display it seemed, Rand followed the direction of Wolf's gaze. His mouth dropped and his eyes widened the moment their gazes met. Obviously the captain didn't expect he'd see her on deck at this early hour of the morning. She couldn't fault him that. Nonetheless, he acknowledged her with a dip of his head and strolled toward her.

"Good morning, Lissa." A boyish grin appeared as he approached. "You don't mind if I call you Lissa, do you? Lissabeth just seems far too formal aboard a ship full of loud, obnoxious, ill-mannered and ill-bred seafarers."

The description of his men as well as himself made her laugh and right now, that sounded foreign and a bit out of place given her circumstances. Still, she shrugged.

"No, I don't mind at all."

"Good." He shot a glance in the direction of his cabin. "I must say I didn't think I'd see you quite this soon. I would've thought that after your—well—I would've thought you'd be taking advantage of a comfortable bed for a while longer. You know, so you could catch up on some much needed sleep. Last night you looked like you could use a solid week's worth, if not a tad more."

"I heard voices," she said. "They sounded quite anxious? Is everything all right?"

"Well, let's see. How do I explain this?" He scratched at the corner of his mustache, dropping his gaze to his boots. "Strange though it may seem, the sudden appearance of a thick fog, combined with an unexpected shift in wind, somehow transported us here."

"Transported us here?" A flush warmed her cheeks.

"Carried us like a slick barrel on the downhill side of ice," he said, as one of his palms slid down over the other. "As a result, my first mate tells me we're at about twenty-two degrees latitude. That's a full degree away from the position we occupied less than half an hour ago."

"Oh. I see. Is this something that alarms you?"

He chuckled. "A full degree, even with a favorable wind, should take us at least six full hours to navigate, Lissa, not mere minutes. In addition, we're now heading in the opposite direction without changing position of sails or rudder. To cap it off, we've no way of rectifying the matter until either the weather calms or our temperamental winds shift their direction yet again. What do you think of that?"

"I don't, um—"

Did she unwittingly move the ship farther than intended and at a distance he would deem impossible? Worse yet, how would the error in judgment affect the rescue of her sister? How far away had she taken them from San Juan? She bit down on the inside of her lip and found the captain staring at her.

"This-this strange occurrence doesn't concern you overly much?"

For a moment Rand said nothing. Just as she opened her mouth to fill the silence, he shook his head.

"Not as much as it might've had the ocean not made me privy to a few of its more mischievous shenanigans over the course of my lifetime."

"Mischievous shenanigans? I'm not sure what you mean."

His gaze took on a distant expression. "Oh, I don't know. Let's just say that I've seen some pretty strange things during the years I've sailed our most unpredictable seas."

She smiled. "Like what?"

"I suppose the one that haunts me most occurred when I served as first mate aboard a ship called the *Vrijheid*. On that fine day we sailed calm, sunny waters. At the time, we were closing in on an enemy ship. With the use of one of our more powerful spy-glasses, I finally had the vessel in my sights. Before I could alert the captain to her position and military strength, a colossal wave—one I would estimate at least eighty feet in height—rose straight up out of the ocean like an enraged goddess looking for retribution. I'd never before seen anything like it. That enormous swell swallowed the ship whole. The vessel never once came up for air. No men, no wreckage, no debris ever surfaced—just gone."

Lissa lowered her lashes and let go of the breath she hadn't known she'd held until that moment. Rand didn't associate the fog or his current position with any of Armando's claims. At least, not yet.

"You needn't worry though," he said. "We'll be all right once we get our bearings."

"I'm not worried. I've no doubt you can command this ship without mishap, *Kapitein*, and far better than most."

"Well, I appreciate the belief you have in me as well as the compliment. Of course, given the situation, this also means you won't be seeing land as soon as either of us expected."

"A voyage aboard your ship, regardless of duration, is preferable to my intended fate aboard the galleon."

Rand settled his gaze on the ocean waves. The comment made the captain uncomfortable. No matter. He'd ask for an explanation soon enough. *He'd have to, wouldn't he?* She grasped the rail and gazed at the white, billowing clouds overhead.

"I don't suppose you know how close we are to land and where on the map that land might be?" she asked.

"Under the current circumstances, I'm afraid I don't have the answer to either question. At least, not yet and not with any degree of certainty."

Her heart tumbled again. What had she done? She must reach San Juan before Margaretha ran out of time. "If such proves the case, then I hope I won't be a burden to either you or your crew."

"You needn't worry over that," he said. "A female presence aboard the *Draeck* is always welcome."

"That's a kind thing for you to say." She paused. "You don't believe a woman aboard a ship brings bad luck, then?"

"Quite the contrary, actually. In all my years at sea, I've never once experienced so much as a shred of truth in that ridiculous notion."

Lissa turned and faced him full on. "All your years? You don't look that old to me, *Kapitein* Van Locken."

"The name is Rand, please. I'm not one for formality, all right?"

She nodded. "If that's what you prefer."

"Not only would I prefer it, I insist."

"So, tell me Rand, did you inherit this ship from a previous captain?" she asked.

"Nay, I didn't. I captained a merchant ship until I saved enough money to purchase this vessel. I had her built to my own specifications, I might add. From that time on, I have had the freedom to make my own choices as to where, why, and when to sail. Now, at least for the time being, I've chosen to sail under the charter of the Dutch West India Company. Once I tire of that, I'll move on."

Her fingertips glided back and forth over the top of the highly polished rail.

"Well, this is a beautiful ship and I must say the figurine of your red painted dragon is most impressive."

His eyes gleamed as he nodded. "Aye, the *Draeck* has been good to me and my men. Very good. In turn, we take great care of her."

"These men here with you now—have they been with you from the moment you took possession of the *Draeck* then?"

"The greater portion of them, aye. With the utmost confidence, I can tell you that you won't find a finer crew sailing the sea today. Their level of skill, loyalty, and courage is unsurpassed. If the need should arise, I wouldn't hesitate to trust any one of them with my life."

A fair-haired, middle-aged man with a cheerful smile approached them. He glanced first at her and then turned his attention toward Rand.

"Sorry for the interruption, *Kapitein*, but Andries wants to know if the lady is ready for her breakfast."

Her hand went to her stomach. She didn't feel the least bit hungry. Not after the amazing feast the cook provided late last night. "Oh. Well, I don't think that I could possibly eat a single bite right now—"

"You should try to eat something anyway, even if just a little bit," Rand said. "You need to regain your strength, Lissa. Really you do."

In reluctant submission, she let go of a soft sigh and nodded. "All right, I'll try to eat a little if you insist."

"I insist." He aimed a thumb at the messenger. "Hazael will accompany you back to my cabin."

Lissa shook her head. "No, that's not at all necessary. I can eat my breakfast out here or even in the galley. I'll not invade your cabin for that. You can just assign me some out-of-the-way place to bide while we find our way to that—"

He placed gentle fingers on top of her lips and shushed her words. "I thought we settled this last night. The cabin is yours for the duration of our voyage. Our current circumstance doesn't change a thing."

"But you'll need access to all of your—"

"Don't worry about what I need. I dare say I'll get along just fine. I'm sure if I need something inside my cabin, you won't mind the intrusion. Now please, go eat some breakfast before you waste away to nothing.

Should that occur, I'll have to live with the memory of your gaunt, paltry form for the rest of my life. You wouldn't want to inflict such an ordeal on me, would you?"

A breath of laughter accompanied the slight shake of her head.

"No, we can't have that, can we?"

"Nay, we can't," he said. "Oh, and when you're finished eating, let Hazael take a look at your wrist. Among other things, he acts as the ship's surgeon."

She nodded. "As you wish, *Kapitein*."

"Rand," he reminded her.

"All right then, as you wish, Rand."

"That's better."

He winked as Hazael put a hand at her back and walked her back to the cabin. While they waited for Andries' arrival, he sat down in the chair beside her and took hold of her injured hand.

The doctor huffed out a scornful breath as he examined the damage around her wrist.

"This Manera, he isn't a very nice man, is he?"

The remark surprised her. Not for the knowledge of her imprisonment, but for the speed at which the details spread given the morning's chaotic events. The memory of her capture flooded her mind, a thing for which she took full responsibility. She'd grown careless. Manera took advantage of, and gloried in, that moment of carelessness.

She had stood in the dark forest behind the citadel more intent on her enchantment than on who or what may have surrounded her. The only thing important to her at that moment was Margaretha's rescue.

Lissabeth shook away the memory. "Benavides

doesn't pay him to be nice. He pays him to produce results. Still, the injury looks far worse than what it is. You needn't worry. It'll heal well enough and I have—"

"Quite possible, but I've a wondrous balm that I implore you to use, nonetheless. At least that way, I'll feel like I'm doing my job. Oh, and it works fairly well on bruises as well," he said as his gaze drifted over the ugly marks on her arms.

"If it pleases you."

"Such will please me well." He gave her hand a tender pat and placed it gently on the table. "So, tell me, what possessed them to lock you up in such a revolting manner anyway?"

As she sought for a reasonable explanation, Andries tapped at the door and entered the room with a tray in hand.

"Ah, your breakfast has arrived." Hazael stood up. Smiling, he bowed as he made room for the cook. "I'll come back with the balm after you've eaten and rested up a bit, hmm?"

"All right. Thank you, Hazael."

"Nay, you needn't thank me. 'Twas my pleasure, I assure you," he called over his shoulder as he closed the door.

"I'm sorry," said Andries as he placed the plate on the table. "I didn't mean to interrupt."

"You didn't. We weren't talking about anything of importance, really. The doctor and I were just chatting."

"Seems that's the goal of every man aboard this ship, Lissabeth." He chuckled as he sat in the seat Hazael had just left. "I give you fair warning, they're lining up at your door."

"I don't mind. I'm sure with the circumstances

surrounding my unexpected arrival I'm a bit of a curiosity. I think it's best to put that curiosity to rest."

Andries cleared his throat in an exaggerated manner. "Yes, well, I must admit I'm a bit curious about that too, what with all the bizarre symbols and such carved into the door. Aye, Laurens told us all about it. I'm burning to know the reason they'd do such a curious thing. But being a bit older and far wiser than my shipmates, I'm of a mind to believe the *kapitein* should be the first to hear your story—should you feel inclined to tell it, that is."

Lissa shrugged. "He hasn't asked."

"Nay, but I wager he will." Andries paused for a moment. "Let me tell you something, Lissabeth. I've sailed with the *kapitein* most all his life. I know him better than most. Rand hasn't asked for an explanation for two reasons. One, he'll not want you further distressed over the memory until he thinks you're somewhat recovered from your ordeal. The second reason stems from the commitment he made to Heyn and the West India Company. The *kapitein* isn't a man who likes to feel divided between honor and duty. However, since we've no idea where we are, or even where *they* are for that matter, he'll ask you soon enough. You can trust me on that."

Lissa glanced down at her smoked bacon and eggs as she picked up her fork. Yes, the captain would ask his questions and sooner rather than later, no doubt. She just didn't know how much to tell him when that moment finally arrived.

****

"I wonder how far off course we are?" Wolf asked as Rand stepped up onto the helm beside him.

"Good question, and it's one I don't have an answer for. I sure would like one though."

"Wouldn't we all?" Wolf faced him. "If the wind simply thrust us a league or two from the main fleet, as one would logically assume, then one would think we'd have found our bearings and Heyn well before now."

"Aye."

"Of course, one also must wonder why we're the only ship affected by the force of that mysterious wind. Should it not have carried the other ships away as well and in the same direction as us?"

"I've asked that same question a thousand times and haven't found an answer yet."

"So then, what do you think happened to us out there?"

"I don't have the slightest idea," Rand replied. "Never in all my days have I heard a sailor speak of such a thing. Not even when they spouted their wildest tales and were well into their cups."

"Well, I figured if anyone had a tall tale that'd make sense of all this, it'd be you," said Wolf.

"Tall tales generally have a reasonable explanation, if one can find it."

"Therein lays the trouble, right?" Wolf cocked his head toward Rand's cabin. "So, my friend, what will you do with Lissabeth now since handing her off to Heyn is no longer an option?"

Rand gazed toward the horizon. For a time he watched the gentle swell of ocean waves as he mulled over the dilemma. "I don't know. At least, not yet."

"Nay? Is there a reason for that?"

He shook his head. "There's far more we must consider now that we've the time to do it. I don't think it wise to drop her off at the first harbor we find or provide passage onboard another ship in the destination of her choice. At least, not without having the answers to some questions first."

"Such as?"

"Such as why did the Spaniards lock her in chains when she hadn't the smallest chance of escape? Where were they taking her? What did they intend to do with her once they arrived at their destination? Her manner of dress doesn't indicate a family of great wealth or position. So I can't imagine they planned a ransom or needed her for some unknown political purpose."

"I agree. Nonetheless, they must've imprisoned her onboard the galleon for a reason. If Manera is to be believed, they thought she had some sort of unearthly power. A power they feared, according to Laurens."

Rand snorted his contempt. "Or so Manera claimed. He may've conjured such a lie, so we'd keep her onboard the galleon where they could carry out whatever hideous plan he and the captain might've concocted. At any rate, I feel I must discover the truth of the matter before we abandon her on some island without any protection whatsoever."

"We can't in good conscious do otherwise."

Rand sighed as he nodded. "I haven't delved into the matter with her yet. I didn't have the heart. If you could've seen her inside that filthy berth, Wolf. She looked so pathetic, so pale and thin. Her eyes carried this haunted look. As long as I live, I shall never forget it. 'Twas like she carried a heavy weight she shouldn't have had to carry. Then when I discovered those bruises about her arms and shoulders, I thought perhaps they'd used the girl for sport. Yet, when I asked Lissa about the possibility she said they hadn't. For the contemptuous look in her eyes, I believed her. I suppose we should be grateful they didn't add such to the torment she had already endured."

"What if those bizarre symbols and plant matter about the door served as some kind of peculiar means to terrify her? What it they were meant to repress her spirit, or even in some twisted way, bend her to their will? Make her believe they had some kind of power over her?" Wolf asked. "Suggestion can be a powerful thing. Especially after one has been kept in dark isolation for an extended period of time."

"Very possible. The Spaniards could come up with something like that. Especially in the treatment of a perceived slave, if that's what they intended her fate should be. There's one more thing we must consider as well."

"Such as?"

"Now that she's escaped them, do you think they'll employ any and all means to get her back?"

A hardened glint filled Wolf's eyes. "If such is their intention, they won't find success."

'Nay, upon my word, they won't."

Wolf raked a hand across his beard as he regarded him. "You know, had I been the one to discover the girl in that berth, I'm not so sure I'd have been as kind to Manera as you were. You're a finer man than I am, Rand."

Rand blew out a scornful breath. "Kindness had nothing to do with it, trust me. I wanted that man to experience, firsthand, what Lissa had endured during her imprisonment. I wanted him to feel the same terror and pain she surely felt while locked inside that dank, filthy hole. After that, Heyn could do with him as he pleased."

Wolf nodded but said nothing in response.

Hendrick approached. "I finished the inventory of our supplies, *Kapitein*, just as you asked."

"What's your best estimate?" Rand exchanged a glance with Wolf.

Supplies were low. Too low. If all had gone according to plan, they would've resupplied the ship in Cuba once they conquered the Benavides fleet. The mysterious fog that had enshrouded them had changed all that.

"The food should last at least another five, maybe six days if we ration it," Hendrick replied. "The water? Maybe four days if we're careful."

"All right. Make sure the men don't mention the need for rationing around Lissa. If she gets wind of it, she probably won't eat or drink the quantity she needs. Right now she needs a great deal of both food and water."

"Aye, *Kapitein*, I'll let them know straightaway."

"In the meantime, take the empty barrels up on deck so we can collect every drop of rain that falls between here and the next place we drop anchor."

"Aye, *Kapitein*." Hendrick hastened to his duty.

Wolf cleared his throat in an exaggerated manner and leaned toward him. "Well, let's hope that rain arrives sooner rather than later, shall we?"

Rand chuckled as he again scanned the horizon for any sign of land. "Aye and sooner would suit me just fine."

Chapter Four

On her third full day aboard the ship, the enchanting strains of a fiddle silenced her troubled thoughts. Lissa left the solitude of the captain's cabin and followed the sound. She ventured toward the top deck in search of the musician whose talent rivaled that of her dear papa. The early afternoon sun and a gentle breeze caressed her face. Both acted as a much needed balm to her tattered soul.

Lissa inhaled a deep breath of the salty sea air while the music flowed into her ears. Her gaze drifted over each member of Rand's crew. They were all the finest of men, of this she was certain. Her judgment of character 'twas a gift inherited from her mother. Honorable men though they all were, she didn't know if she could or even should seek their help. She didn't know if she could trust them with her most guarded secret either. At least not yet. Perhaps what she needed was more time in their company.

Antonis sat by the foremast, instrument in hand. The sweet harmony that called her from her borrowed berth soon gave way to a livelier tune. Broad smiles appeared in response to the song. The crewmen clapped their hands and stomped their feet to the beat of the music. At the same time they sang the words. The deep resonance of their collected voices thrilled her no end. She moved closer still.

"Hey now, mind the words," Andries bellowed out the moment he spied her. "We have a lady present."

Joris captured her gaze and then rose to his feet. The mischief sparkling from his eyes, as well as the grin, begged full release. He danced toward her then took firm hold of her hand. He hummed the tune as he swept her into his arms and led her to the center of the deck where they had more room. Whistles and cheers accompanied their dance.

The moment the song ended, Laurens stepped between them. "I'm claiming a dance if you don't mind. So, move aside, my friend, before you get caught up in the melee."

Lissa laughed over Laurens's smirk and Joris's frown. He muttered something under his breath about minding very much and how nice it would be if some people aboard the ship would strive for a little more consideration.

"Ah, don't mind him," said Laurens. "He's a bit crabby when he doesn't get his way. However, 'twas my good intention to come swiftly to your rescue since the man can be rather clumsy at times. Therefore, I didn't want your feet to suffer."

"I'm not sure you're the one who should mention such an affliction," Joris shot back. "Might I remind you of the incident inside that little pub in New Amsterdam? Why, the poor wench will never be the same again. Never."

"You know, he's right about that, Laurens." Johannes chortled. "As I recall, you had the entire establishment in an uproar the minute your foot knotted in the woman's skirts. Then when you couldn't untangle yourself in time, you dropped that poor girl on her backside. You thus relieved her of all dignity. More than likely you left a bruise or two as well."

"At least he had enough sense to beg the lady's pardon." Pieter's light blue eyes twinkled with mirth. "'Twas his only saving grace."

Uproarious laughter followed the comments. Laurens shrugged them off as he spun her around the deck. Despite the jibes, she found the ship's carpenter an excellent dance partner. Before she could catch her breath, Johannes grabbed her hand and tugged her toward him.

"Take heart, dear lady. I'll save you from Laurens's inept clutches, lest you meet the same fate as that poor girl in the aforementioned pub."

Hazael claimed her hand next. Cornelius soon followed and then Conrad Shaers, the gunner with hazel eyes and dark brown hair. She felt sure that every other member of Rand's crew assigned to the top deck at that hour, danced with her as well. Finally, just as Antonis slowed the tempo of his songs, Wolf took over. Pieter bowed low at the waist. He stepped back and joined his mates in singing the words of the sweet, mournful ballad Antonis now played.

A touch of humor filled the handsome man's eyes as he dropped a hand to her waist and grasped her hand. "You looked like you needed a bit of a rest, so I asked Antonis to slow it down a bit. I hope you don't mind the change in pace."

She laughed as she matched her steps to his, grateful for the rest. "Not at all. In fact, I appreciate it, so thank you very much, kind sir."

"You're most welcome. Now tell me, how are you faring on this fine day?" he asked.

"Quite well. Everyone has been very kind to me since my arrival."

"As well they should. Do you feel as though you have recovered from your recent ordeal then?" he asked.

"Fully recovered. I wished you all wouldn't worry so much about me. Although very endearing, it truly isn't necessary."

"Now, how can we help but worry over such a lovely lady?"

"I don't know, but if you all tried really, really, hard, I bet you could to it," she quipped. "I am hardier than you think."

He threw back his head and laughed. "You are a delight, Lissa. Do you know that? A true delight."

She took in a much needed breath while her gaze wandered over the crew. "The men sing amazingly well. I don't think I've ever heard the like before. Especially, not from the crewmen of a ship."

He nodded. "Gives them something agreeable to do while we pass away the time."

"What? Are you telling me you don't deign to sing along with them?" she teased.

"Rarely," he replied. "I can't carry a tune, and neither can Rand for that matter. We have a few others among our ranks that are tone-deaf as well. As a result, those who sing prefer those of us who don't to shut up and listen. After all, every choir needs an audience, don't you think?"

"Yes, I suppose you're right about that. Trust me; I'm quite happy to join with you as an avid spectator."

****

The ongoing revelry above him urged Rand into

full awareness sooner than he might've liked. Nonetheless, he awoke feeling refreshed and well-rested despite the additional hour or two he might've needed. He left Wolf's cabin, which they now shared in shifts, and climbed the ladder to the foredeck.

Arriving, he caught sight of his first mate holding Lissa close in his arms. They shared laughter and pleasant conversation. That set him back on his heels a step or two. He didn't know why the scene bothered him, but it did. Without giving it any further thought, he ambled toward the couple. He tapped Wolf on the shoulder. The man didn't look the least surprised to see him.

Despite the intrusion, Wolf simply gave him possession of Lissa's hand and then stepped back against the rail. All the while the man sported an annoying smirk. He would gladly have removed it if not for Lissa's presence. Rand ignored the grin. Instead, he concentrated his full attention upon Lissa.

Her eyes filled with vibrant light and a rosy glow touched her cheeks. Both did naught but enhance her beauty. He found it nigh on impossible to take his gaze off her. If he read her blush correctly, his intense gaze discomfited her. As she dropped her gaze, he glanced at his crew.

"For the need to catch up on a bit of sleep, it seems I'm missing out on all the fun up here."

She bit down on her bottom lip as she peeked over at Antonis. "I'm sorry. I hope the music and dancing didn't disturb you too much."

"Not at all. I've grown quite accustomed to the boisterous escapades of my men. Besides, if the need is great enough, I can sleep through almost anything." He paused as he tilted his head from side to the side. "Save cannon fire. More often than not, the deafening roar from the guns rouses me from even my deepest slumber."

She had the charity to laugh over his miserable attempt at humor. "I'm glad to hear it, for most assuredly, your crew wouldn't want you sleeping through an attack."

"Nay, I can't imagine they would."

"Do you all have this kind of gathering often?"

"The music? Aye. The dancing? Not so much," he replied. "But then again, finding such a lovely companion to dance with while aboard the ship is a rather rare occurrence."

"That's a very sweet thing for you to say," she murmured as she gazed at Antonis. "He has quite a talent, doesn't he?"

"Aye, that he does, and believe me, we're all grateful he has it. His music makes the time spent aboard this vessel far more pleasant."

"I can see that, and I must tell you, I'm impressed that he knows so many different songs. To my recollection, he's yet to play the same one twice."

He gave her a sideways glance. "I take it you've been up here awhile then?"

A nod accompanied a captivating smile. He wondered if her misfortune aboard the galleon had begun to fade at last. If so, perhaps he could ask a few of his questions.

"I suppose you could say that. I know I've danced with every member of your crew. At least, those here on deck, anyway."

That ended his thoughts. "I didn't realize. Do you

need to rest?"

"No, I'm all right. Wolf asked Antonis to slow the songs down, so I could catch my breath. The ploy worked like a charm."

"I'm not surprised he did so," he muttered. The thought rankled. Did his first mate truly worry over Lissa's need for rest or want to hold her a bit closer than protocol dictated with a livelier tune? And by all the saints, why did it matter either way?

The moment they completed their second dance, he slipped one hand about her waist and dropped the other to his side. "Would you like a moment away from all this?"

"Yes, I think I might, if you don't mind."

"I don't mind at all." He led her toward the crates near the galley doorway. "Andries? Fetch Lissa some water, will you please? She looks like she could use it."

"Aye, *Kapitein*. More than that, I think she needs something in her belly. As luck would have it, supper should be just about ready."

The announcement ended the music fest. At once his men fanned out in search of a place to eat their evening meal.

"It's such a beautiful evening, I think I'll eat up here with you and your crew this evening, if that's all right with you, of course," she said.

"That's fine by me. Andries did you hear that? The lady will dine with us."

Andries waved an amiable hand as he headed down the steps leading to the galley. "Aye that I did. I'll return shortly with meal in hand, so don't go anywhere."

Rand settled in beside her. "I didn't thank you for

the dances. I rather enjoyed them."

"You needn't thank me. After all, it provided a bit of fun." She chewed on a nail and then dropped her hand in her lap. "Now that I think on it, it's been quite a while since I last had the opportunity to dance," she added.

"I'm sorry to hear that. You should be given frequent opportunities to use your skill." She did dance very well. As well as any woman in any court or high society he had ever seen. She didn't dance like a peasant.

Lissa shrugged. "In truth, dancing really isn't that high on my list of priorities."

"Is it not? I find that quite unusual for a woman your age." He found many things unusual about this woman. Just who was she? More than ever, he wanted his answers. Where to begin? "Well then, if not one of your priorities, how did you learn to dance with such grace and elegance?"

Murmuring her thanks, she accepted the bowl of hearty beef stew, thick with carrots and potatoes. Andries then handed the captain his meal.

"Oh, I don't know about the grace, but dancing is a frequent activity in the village I come from, just as it is in most I suppose. In such places, one is expected to join in the revelry."

"You know, I find that interesting," he said between bites.

She drew her brows together. "Interesting? I don't know what you mean. Didn't you dance where you came from?"

"No, it isn't that. It's just that the way you dance rivals any I've seen in the highest levels of any society

I've ever visited. Therefore if asked, I would've presumed you were a regular guest at their frequent functions."

She laughed quietly. "Oh no, not me. But you make it sound as if you've attended such gatherings often enough and found them lacking."

He shrugged. "Let's just say I've seen more than my fair share of festive occasions devised by the so-called aristocracy. With my father's position in the Dutch admiralty, such was inevitable I suppose."

"You don't enjoy their social gatherings?"

He leaned toward her and grinned. "In truth, I don't know a single male worth his salt who truly does. Personally, I would rather navigate the great banks of the North Sea. I'd willingly do it during a raging storm—and blindfolded at that—just to avoid such an affair."

She laughed. "The North Banks? You know, I've heard about those banks on many different occasions since I was a little girl. Are they really all that bad?"

"They can be."

"And here I thought it was just tall tales."

She had a gleam in her eyes as she tilted her head to the side. Her lips parted as she drew her brows slightly together. What did that look mean? She opened her mouth to speak. Then, as if she thought better of it, she closed it again.

"Nay, we'll have none of that. Please go ahead and say it, or ask it, as the case might be."

"Oh, it's nothing really. I just wondered if you were one of those seafarers who invoke the protection of Nehalennia before you make such a crossing."

"Nehalennia?"

"The ancient goddess who protects voyagers while they sail across the North Sea. I can't imagine you haven't heard of her. Most Dutch sailors have."

"Hmm. You know, I think I do have a vague memory of the tale."

"Tale, *Kapitein* Van Locken?" She glanced at him sideways. "Despite the ocean's mischievous shenanigans—which you say you've witnessed yourself—are you not a sailor who believes in the deep-rooted legends of the sea?"

"Nay, I can't say that I am."

"Does that include the existence of the Undines then?"

He shook his head. "The what?"

"You know, the sea nymphs. Sirens?" She raised a brow. "Mermaids?"

He laughed out loud at the question. "As much as I'd like to report otherwise, I haven't seen a single one myself. Therefore, I can't attest to their existence."

"I see."

The look that entered her eyes gave him pause.

"Have you ever seen one?"

"No, but did you know that according to all reports, Christopher Columbus swore that he saw three of them at once?"

He set his empty bowl off to the side. "Did he now?"

She nodded. "The man recorded the account in his journal, or so they say. If I remember correctly, he said the nymphs rose up out of the water. In his opinion, they were not half as comely as the various paintings he'd seen throughout his lifetime. In fact, he thought their faces looked far more masculine than they did feminine. In addition to his testimony, a man sailing with Henry Hudson said he saw one as well. His mermaid had pale skin from the navel up and long, black hair. As I recall the story, the moment she leaped back into the ocean, he spied the fish tail that made up the rest of her body." Her eyes danced with merriment. "Are you sure you've never seen one? After all, some of the stories do come from reputable men."

"Nay, nothing even remotely close."

"Well, that's probably a good thing. I hear such creatures lure men to their deaths."

Long after Lissa sought her bed, he realized he hadn't reaped a shred of information concerning her past or current circumstances. The subject of her captivity aboard the galleon remained distant. Instead of the answers he sought, they had whiled away the evening hours talking about trivial things. He hadn't intended it to be so. Happenstance? Or did she steer the conversation away from herself deliberately?

With ale in hand, Wolf plopped down beside him. "What's the matter? The evening didn't go quite the way you planned it?"

"What are you talking about?"

"Oh, I don't know, you just seem a little glum," he replied. "I thought perhaps your evening spent in Lissa's company didn't go quite the way you hoped it might. You know, regarding your pursuit of the girl."

"What are you blathering on about, man? Speak your mind."

Wolf shrugged as he swigged from his tankard. "If you wish to pretend you don't have anything more than a passing interest in Lissa, that's fine by me. I can go along with it. For now, anyway."

Rand met the mirthful gaze head on. "What makes you think my interest in Lissa is anything more than that of a passenger aboard my ship, in need of help?"

The annoying smirk returned, followed by outright laughter as he rose to his feet. Wolf patted his shoulder.

"Perhaps I'll let you think on that while I go below and get some sleep. Mayhap come the morning you'll have an answer."

Chapter Five

Bursts of lightning lit up the clouds and painted them in vibrant, vivid colors she'd never before seen. Bolt after flaming bolt struck the ocean in a never-ending brutal assault. The deafening roar of thunder blended with each flash of blinding light. The fury of the tempestuous winds created enormous waves that moaned as they battered the solitary vessel that sailed upon the sea.

Wolf braced himself as he stood at the helm of that ship and called out orders. The men onboard obeyed without question as they battled the storm in a fearsome brawl for life over death.

But where was Rand? She gazed all about the deck of the ship and couldn't find him. Wait! The ship didn't look like the Rood Draeck.

Suddenly thick black clouds engulfed the brigantine. Despite every skill Wolf and his men possessed, the ship and all her occupants were at the mercy of the raging storm.

Strange swirling lights slithered from out of the ocean then and climbed aboard the vessel. 'Twas almost as if they had a life of their own. The vibrant beams shrieked ominous sounds each time they bounced off the ship's deck. Those lights scattered in all directions despite the course of the wind. Monstrous waves flung men overboard with heartbreaking ease.

Then a swirling vortex formed, possessing the ship. There was nothing more Wolf could do but hold on tight, and her heart ached for him. The mist tossed the brigantine across time and space though a gate created entirely by thick dark clouds.

Yet, the bluest sky she'd ever seen glimmered at portal's end—

Lissa gasped as she opened her eyes. *What in Heaven's name did I just see?*

Her heart raced as she relived the amazing vision many times over. Did the ship belong to Wolf and was he her captain? Whether he owned the ship or not, she knew the event would happen in the not-too-distant future. After all, Wolf didn't look very much older, if any older at all.

Nonetheless, the things she saw filled her with an overwhelming sense of awe and wonder. The foreknowledge also filled her with sorrow for the lives lost. None of her past visions could compare. Yet, if she shared what she had just foreseen with Wolf, he would think her quite insane. So, most likely, would Rand, ocean shenanigans or no shenanigans.

Regardless of the way he might perceive what she saw and whether he believed her or not, should she at least warn him of the danger ahead? What could she say, really? She had no idea where or when that storm would occur. Wolf was not a man who would cease sailing just because he would encounter a storm in an unknown day or time, regardless of its devastating strength, would he?

She sighed. *Storms.*

She'd seen her fair share of them throughout her life. All the occupants aboard the *Rood Draeck* would face a pretty fierce one today. But then they'd also find the land the captain so diligently sought. She knew he worried over their dwindling supplies, though he didn't want her knowing about that. With the coming tempest, not only could the captain resupply his ship, he would also know exactly where they were. That knowledge would bring them all the closer to the rescue of Margaretha *if* he chose to help her. She still didn't know if she should ask.

"Lissa? Are you dressed?"

Lissa swung her legs over the side of the bed. She smoothed away the wrinkles from her skirt and tamed the tangles in her hair as best she could with the tips of her fingers. "Yes, you can come in."

Rand flashed a charming grin as he entered the room. "If you've no objections, I thought I would catch up on my logbook this morning. I've neglected it of late and since all is quiet right now, I have the perfect opportunity to remedy that."

She swept a hand toward the table. "Help yourself. This is your cabin after all. If you'll excuse me, I'll just leave you in peace while you—"

"Nay, don't do that. In fact, it would please me if you'd stay. This isn't something that takes a great deal of concentration or effort, so I welcome your company."

"All right then, if you insist."

"Insist is a little harsh. How about we call it an invitation I'd like you to accept?"

He retrieved his book, ink well, and quill from the first narrow drawer across from his bunk and spread them out across the table. He held her chair as she slipped into the one just opposite his.

"What type of things do you put in there?" she asked.

"Just the day to day proceedings concerning the ship and her crew—weather, position, inventory, that sort of thing," he said as he sat down and scooted his chair forward.

A smile emerged despite her best effort to avoid its escape. "So, how will you explain the events and current position of your ship? They were expecting you to meet up with the Dutch fleet, after all."

Rand flipped through the pages, found the one he needed and then dipped his quill into the inkwell. He winked.

"Well, I can't blame it on mermaids. However, we did have some unusual weather, and I've a host of witnesses to that fact. No one can refute the claim even if they tried."

She laughed but offered nothing more in return.

"Besides, no one looks at these logs anyway. Unless, of course, an unfortunate incident occurs that warrants the intrusion. Most captains I know are rather careless about keeping them for that very reason." He shrugged. "I suppose that keeping mine so studiously stems from my father's arduous training."

"Do you also keep an inventory of all the treasures you discover on enemy ships?"

"Yes, I do, and a careful inventory at that. I wouldn't want anyone to think we were keeping more than the share we agreed upon."

"Does that include one rescued, bedraggled prisoner of the Spaniards?"

Lissa hoped that her smile and light-hearted tone would give Rand leave to finally ask his questions.

He sat back in his chair as they gazed at each other. Seconds passed without either of them saying a word. Finally he extended his arm across the table and took hold of her hand.

"Can you tell me about that, Lissa?"

She dropped her gaze as she lifted a shoulder. "I'm not sure where to even start—"

A knock at the door interrupted her thoughts.

"Aye?" Rand called out.

Andries opened the door a crack. "Wolf needs you top-side, *Kapitein*, if you can spare a moment?"

Lissa waved a hand and smiled as he muttered a curse underneath his breath. "Please go on. Duty calls and you must answer."

****

Once he left his cabin, Rand headed straight for the foredeck, pondering his brief conversation with Lissa and all the things she might've told him. If not for the urgency in Andries' voice, he would've remained in his cabin until the end of her tale.

"Looks like we have us a storm brewing, *Kapitein*," Wolf said.

Rand fixed his gaze toward the thick, dark clouds gathering in the distance and nodded. "Aye, and from the looks of things, it's certain to be a brutal one."

"What do you think, about two, perhaps three hours before we hit a top sail gale?" he asked.

"Assuming luck is on our side, we'll get all of three. In the meantime, have Cornelius batten down the hatches in the event it's less than half that and call all hands on deck."

"Already taken care of. He's gathering the men as we speak," Wolf replied.

"You're a good man, Wolf." Rand patted his shoulder. With a devilish grin he exaggerated the clearing of his throat. "I've taught you well and I'm thinking you should thank me for that."

Wolf chuckled. "That you have, my friend. That you have, and I do thank you for it."

"Well, with that being said—if you haven't already by now—my advice is that you turn your thoughts toward commanding a ship of your own. You're more than ready and have been for quite some time. I also know for the wages I've paid you, you've accumulated more than enough gold to purchase or build any vessel you like," he said.

"I'll take that as a fine compliment, and when I feel the time is right, I'll heed your advice."

"Don't let your loyalty to me get in the way of your future, Wolf. Though admirable, I will not hesitate to terminate you from my service and personally escort you off my ship if you linger too long. You can trust me on that."

"I'll be sure to keep that in mind as well. But now that you've brought up the subject of escorting individuals off the ship, might I ask if you've made a decision concerning Lissa?" said Wolf.

"A decision?"

"Aye. One might think that by now, you've arrived at some sort of decision concerning the girl and her desires. Yet, you've said nary a word as to your course."

A bit of jealousy took possession of him the moment Wolf mentioned Lissa. For the umpteenth time he recalled the way his first mate held her in his arms as they danced. At once he banished it as ridiculous.

"We've not spoken of it yet," Rand said. "So, I suppose we'll keep her with us until we find out just where it is she wants to go. But, until we know where we are, I can't very well chart a course for her desired destination, now can I?"

Wolf raised an incredulous brow. "Really? In all your conversations with the girl, you've still not asked why the Spaniards held her captive or where home is?"

"Nay, not as yet." He left it at that.

"Well, if I were you, I wouldn't put it off much longer. She might think you don't care and should the notion settle in her mind, she won't give up a single word. Now, unless you've further orders, I'll go get some sleep before that storm hits."

Wolf's comments echoed inside his mind long after his first mate went below deck for some much needed rest. Rand didn't know why he'd put off seeking answers to his nagging questions until this morn. She seemed quite willing to answer them and he didn't want her changing her mind now. He went straightway toward his cabin, only to spy Lissa standing against the rail near the stern. Her hand clutched her curious pendant as she gazed toward the horizon. She jumped as he appeared.

"I'm sorry. I didn't mean to startle you."

She shook her head and gulped. "You didn't, not really."

He glanced up at the dark, angry clouds that filled the sky. "Are you concerned about the storm?"

"Not at all. Why do you ask?"

"You looked a bit pensive." When she offered nothing in response he launched into his purpose. "If not the storm, would that look have anything to do with your ordeal at the hands of the Spaniards?"

The slightest of smiles lifted the corners of her full lips. "Perhaps if one dug deep enough, one might find a connection."

He took in a breath and then let it go. "What happened, Lissa? Where did you come from? Why did they take you and imprison you aboard that galleon?"

Uncertainty filled her beautiful eyes. She hesitated for just a moment then lifted her chin. He braced himself for what she might say.

"I'm afraid you can't listen to a full explanation right now, Rand, we don't have the time. We can talk this evening, and I promise I'll answer all of your questions then."

He drew his brows together. Of all the unexpected— "Time? What are you talking about? We've nothing but time—"

"*Kapitein*!" With the telescope anchored against his eye, Hendrick waved an excited hand from atop the crow's nest. "We've a small flock of birds flying off the starboard beam. Do you see them? Can't be sure, but they look like egrets and by all the saints, they're leading the way in. If we're lucky, we'll find the shore before the storm overtakes us."

Excited chatter followed the revelation. Rand whirled around in search of the flock heading for their shelter.

"Set your course to the flight of those birds Joris, and steady as she goes. Hendrick, keep him informed."

"Aye, *Kapitein*," they both said in unison.

Without the need for command, every man aboard his ship emerged on deck, fanned out, and manned their posts. During the clamor, Lissa turned toward his cabin.

He leaned forward, grabbed her hand, and drew her back to his side. "You needn't go unless you want to. You're not in the way."

She peeked at him through her lashes. "Well, if you're sure you don't mind. The cabin is a little stuffy right now."

"Then stay. Please."

Her cryptic comment about the lack of time never strayed far from his mind as he took command of the ship. She couldn't possibly have seen the birds; she hadn't even glanced in their direction until Hendrick made his announcement. Even if she had, would she have understood what the sighting meant?

Then at long last, the young crewman let out another whoop of excitement. "Land-ho, *Kapitein*, and I've got good news! I see the island of the flamingos, where food is plentiful and fresh water abounds. We're now heading straight for the southwestern tip."

A mixture of relief and anticipation overtook all else. From this island he could chart a course to any harbor he might choose, for he knew it well.

"Make for the bay, Joris. Cornelius, furl the gallant and top sails. We'll bring her in slow. Antonis, take soundings on approach."

"Aye, *Kapitein*."

Antonis readied his lead and dropped it into the ocean. As they drew close to the island, he called out his readings every couple of minutes.

"Now at six fathoms, *Kapitein* and awaiting your orders."

"Haul wind and lie-to," Rand bellowed. "Secure all sails, drop anchor, and lower the boats. Let's replenish the water and take on fresh provisions while the weather allows. Lissa, would you like some shore time despite the impending storm, or would you rather stay onboard and avoid the deluge?"

"I think I'd rather take advantage of what the island has to offer, if you don't mind," she said. "Besides, I've never minded getting wet."

He extended his hand in invitation. "Then come on."

Within the hour, they rowed for the island, with Wolf at the oars and their boat in the lead. Just as they drew near, Rand saw a shadowy flash of movement from the corner of his eye.

An enormous spotted stingray—larger than any he had ever seen—leaped over the boat. The poisonous spine at the end of its long tail swept downward, piercing Wolf's forearm as the creature dove back into the ocean.

Lissa gasped and bounded to her feet. Using the hem of her skirt, she yanked the barb from the gaping wound. Wolf grimaced in pain, dropped the oars, and planted his hand over the injury.

Rand stood helpless near his friend. Lissa brushed Wolf's hand away and guarded the ugly gash with her own.

"No, Wolf! We need the blood to flow freely. Through it we'll remove as much of the poison as we can." She spared Rand a glance. "We must get him to shore as fast as we can. Time means everything right now."

Joris grabbed the abandoned oars and rowed toward the shore. Rand half-dragged, half-carried Wolf to the shelter of a large tree just as huge drops of rain pounded the earth.

Lissa shook her head. "This won't do. I'll need a fire."

Johannes pinned his gaze to Rand's. "*Kapitein*, that cave we sheltered in once before, it isn't far."

Wolf took in a ragged breath. "I can… I can make it, Rand."

"All right. Let's go."

With grim determination, they hauled Wolf inside the cave at Lissa's direction. She knelt at Wolf's side the moment they had him settled. Despite his pain, her fingers kneaded the skin around the wound, encouraging more blood flow. A shudder passed through his body as he groaned in response.

"I'm so sorry, but this is necessary, Wolf. I wouldn't cause you pain if I didn't have to," she murmured. "I must soak his arm with warm water, Rand, and the sooner the better. Every second, and I mean *every* second, counts. Did you perchance bring something so I can warm up the water I'll need?"

"Aye, I'll have one of the men fetch you something you can use," he said and headed for the cave entrance.

"Wolf, take deep breaths; you must relax your muscles as best you can." Lissa said gently.

Rand took comfort in both the tone and the obvious skill she possessed. The toxin of a stingray could easily kill a man. He'd witnessed that many times over and prayed he wouldn't again. Not when it would take the best friend he had on this earth.

"I've got some of the men gathering firewood, *Kapitein*, they'll return as fast as they can," said Joris. "The trick is in finding wood dry enough for a fire."

"I know. Besides the wood, Lissa needs water and a pot, a cup, or something she can put over a fire. Fetch something suitable as quickly as you can. Wolf's life depends upon speed."

"I'll be right back."

Once Joris disappeared from sight, Rand entered the cave, intending to clear space to build that fire.

A roaring fire already blazed.

Chapter Six

Rand stared at her. Lissa knew that without even turning around. Yet, she wouldn't have chanced exposing her skills right now if it hadn't been necessary. Wolf's injury made it vital, for she couldn't halt the path of the venom if the poison was left unrestrained. No power on earth could do that. She didn't have time for Rand's crew to find dry wood and build a fire in the usual way.

Though fearing what she might see in his eyes, she gathered her courage, and met the captain's gaze head on. The horror, even disgust she expected, didn't appear. She saw nothing more in his eyes than a need for understanding. For a moment, they simply looked at each other.

"Well, at least you haven't hauled me outside and tied me to the stake."

A quiet chuckle accompanied the slight shake of his head. He hunkered down beside her. Wolf had lapsed into blissful unconsciousness.

"Do you think he'll make it through this?"

"Yes."

"You sound confident."

"I am. I'll not let him die."

Rand gazed at the fire. Where had his thoughts taken him? For a while he watched the flames.

"How did you do that?"

Before she could open her mouth, Conrad, Hendrick, Pieter, and Johannes returned with armloads of wood. They immediately fed the blaze as if it had just taken hold and needed a quick refuel before it burned itself out. Then Joris and Cornelius arrived, carrying small pots of water.

"I hope this will do," said Joris.

Lissa nodded. "Thank you and right now it'll do just fine. I may need more water later on, though."

"Don't worry, we'll keep you supplied," Cornelius replied.

"Do you need anything else?" asked Rand.

"Some blankets," she said as she placed both pots close to the fire. "Not only for Wolf, but for everyone else who'll stay on the island tonight. Before he can leave this cave, Wolf will need some recovery time. Two and perhaps even three days if the venom traveled farther than I had hoped."

"We'll fetch the necessary supplies, *Kapitein*," said Joris.

With a forward wave of his hand Joris summoned his companions and strode out of the cavern. Rand leaped to his feet and followed them as far as the entrance. He hollered but with the roar of the wind and the rain she couldn't make out a single word. Not that it mattered right now. The only thing that mattered was Wolf. She would much rather he keep his appointment with that ruthless storm than die here on this island.

Lissa grabbed her petticoat, ripped off a generous piece of the cleanest material, and sopped it into the water. She laid the saturated cloth on top of the wound and let it soak, repeating the process every few minutes over the next several hours.

Once the cloth grew cold, she dropped it back into the pot and examined the blue and purple swelling that surrounded the laceration. The color didn't bode well. Infection would soon set in. She needed more than hot water, she needed leopard's bane, sweet broom, and juniper berries to name a few. Only one choice remained, one she knew she must take despite all consequences.

She glanced at Rand. He and his men were still engaged in conversation. Perhaps they worried over Wolf and discussed his chances for survival? If so, that just might give her enough time. She clutched her talisman tight to her breast, closed her eyes, and waited for the crystal's awakening. Within seconds its brilliant blue light filled her with an abundance of energy. Placing her free hand just above his injury, she transferred that energy into Wolf's body. A thick, rust-colored substance oozed out from the ragged flesh. Once it ran clear of venom, she cleansed the wound and then replaced the cloth.

"Lissa, we must have that talk you promised we'd have. I need it right now."

She froze. His tone made it clear he'd just witnessed the entire event.

"I'll answer all of your questions as best I can and with the honesty I promised. All you need do is ask them. Fair enough?"

He seated himself on the boulder lodged between her and the fire. For a few minutes, silence filled the space between them.

"I don't really know what I should ask, nor do I have any reasonable order to my questions," he said. "Please, just help me understand all of this. You can give me that, can't you?"

How to explain? Yet, before she could summon a single word, Wolf stirred. He put a hand on his chest and shuddered. She cupped his face and then gently caressed his cheek with her thumb.

"Wolf, can you hear me?"

"Aye…"

"Are you nauseated or are you having any difficulty breathing right now?"

He shook his head. "Nay, just a bit of… pain. That's all…"

"I'm so sorry about the pain. There's nothing I can do about that but tell you it will soon pass."

Wolf grabbed her hand, peered at her through lowered lids, and nodded. "Thanks Lissa… and you don't have to answer Rand's questions… if you don't want to. None of his bloody business…," he murmured.

"No, it's all right. He deserves the answers to his questions. In fact, everyone aboard the *Draeck* deserves them," she replied.

"What do you mean?" asked Rand.

"There's a decision you must make, and it should be one you all make together. Now is as good a time as any to provide the details. After all, we'll be here awhile."

Rand rested his loosely clasped hands on top of his thighs and leaned toward her. "We've a decision to make? Concerning what?"

"Me."

"Would you explain a little more fully what you mean by that?"

"Once I do, you might find you just want to leave me here. I wouldn't blame you for that. Therefore, you—"

"I would never abandon you. Not for any reason. Nonetheless, I would still like an explanation."

"Then where shall I begin," she murmured. "Tell me, Rand, given your lack of regard for superstitions and myths, do you know anything at all about the *Witte Wieven*?"

He stiffened and his eyes widened. Under different circumstances his bewilderment might've made her laugh.

"Are you speaking of the "wise women" of ancient Germanic legend?"

"Yes, I am."

He relaxed a bit as he shook his head. "Not much really, just a story here and there. If I remember correctly, during their mortality these fanciful, so called ghost-witches or Elven beings had the gift of prophecy or some other such nonsense. Some people believed that once they died, their spirits possessed a form of magical power to either assist or obstruct those they encountered. There are some who revered them because of that assistance. On the other hand, there were those who abhorred them if they suffered various maladies under the witches' wrath. Not surprisingly, the latter said they should be avoided at all cost." He shrugged. "That's about the sum total of what I know. Why do you ask?"

She shook her head ever so slightly and sighed. "Witches—"

"The term displeases you. Why?"

"Legends are curious things, aren't they," she said more to herself than she did to him. "They only touch on corners of truth and then on nothing more than a whim to embellish or destroy, people alter them beyond all recognition."

"Corners of truth? What are you trying to tell me, Lissa? Please, for the love of heaven, just come out and say whatever it is you must say. I promise you, I'll listen."

"That all the *Witte Wieven* legends you've just mentioned have a foundation based in fact. The stories began centuries ago in Gelderland, the place where I was born and raised. A group of women, all related by blood, settled there during the elder days. Rather than hags or sorceresses, these women and all their female descendants were renowned herbalists and healers, not witches. People would travel great distances in order to obtain a cure for their afflictions. Those that believe in this gift still do to this day. To my knowledge, the *Wieven* never turned away a soul that had a genuine need.

"Most of these women have what you might refer to as magical ability for what you cannot understand, and some more so than others. Although each woman learns to use the natural elements of the earth, as well as the energy that surrounds these elements, individual skill varies. In addition, they are in fact, gifted with the ability to see future events. Again, some to a greater degree than others."

"Oh, come on, Lissa," said Rand. "Surely, you don't believe that."

"Yes, actually, I do." She paused for a moment and then took in a deep breath. "You see, I believe it, Rand, because I am one."

He drew his brows together. "You are one what?"

"A descendant of the *Witte Wieven* who has inherited *all* of the abilities of her ancestors."

There. Her secret was out. For a moment he said nothing. He simply stared at her for what seemed an inordinate amount of time.

"You can't be serious," he said.

"I'm afraid I'm dead serious."

"You think you're some sort of—of Elven being or ghost with magical powers? Because if you truly do, then—"

A breath of laughter escaped her lips. "An Elf? Not hardly. One of the ghost-*wieven*? I'm not that either. At least, not yet. What I am is a very mortal human who possesses the skill to do what *some* might consider some very extraordinary things by natural—not unearthly magical or demonic—means."

His jaw clenched. "That's why you knew we couldn't speak of this earlier today. You already knew we were close to the island," he stated matter-of-factly.

She nodded.

"But then, *if* what you say *is* true—and *if* you can see into the future—how did Benavides and Manera manage to capture you? Why didn't you just elude them with your so-called gift of prophecy?"

"Visions don't work that way, Rand. I can't make them happen at will. In addition, I have no control over the things I see or when I see them. They just occur and when they do, they are rarely complete. I must make sense of them from everything else that surrounds me or from a vision previously seen. There are also times those visions will abruptly change course."

"That doesn't make sense. Why would they change if you're seeing the future?"

"Because the future is never absolute. People can and do have a change of heart. They often regret a decision or simply choose a different path. They can do it all on a whim and in a moment of time. At times these changes will alter their, or someone else's, fate. I bet if you think about it for a moment you'll remember an incident wherein you had something planned—maybe even something important—and then simply changed your mind at the last possible moment."

Wolf grimaced. "That's happened more times than we can count. Right, Rand?"

Rand nodded. "So, you're saying then these revelations of yours never revealed anything concerning Benavides or Manera?"

"Not directly, and not in regard to my capture. Yet, days after they whisked me aboard the galleon, I saw the future he intended for me."

"Exactly what *were* his intentions?"

"To gift "the woman with extraordinary abilities" to the king of Spain. One that could change the fortunes of his kingdom for the better and for many years to come. All by providing him visions of the future. Benavides supposed that such a gift would elevate his status at court. Right now, the man isn't very well thought of, as you might suspect. Once he returns to Spain without ships or treasure, the king will have him imprisoned."

"This impending imprisonment is knowledge gained from a vision you've had?"

"Yes and just because you thwarted his plans by taking me off the ship doesn't mean Benavides will abandon his goal. He'll ask Armando Manera to find me if he hasn't already. In his mind, handing me over to the king is the only way to accomplish an honorable release and ultimately save his life. In turn, Manera will not rest until he fulfills this duty, for he is beholden to the man."

With nothing more she could offer, Lissa focused her attention on Wolf's care. Once again, she removed the cloth from the wound and dropped it into the simmering water. She checked for fever and found none. A sense of relief filled her. Nonetheless, she would still collect some of the medicinal flora this island offered and brew a tea that would heal any internal injury Wolf may have sustained from the venom.

****

Rand chucked another log into the fire. Not that it needed it. His lovely lady "witch" could somehow keep it going without additional wood, could she not? For a while he did naught but observe the tender ministrations she bestowed upon his first mate. It made him a bit envious. For a small, absurd moment, he wished the stingray's barb had fallen upon him instead of Wolf. Then he would know her gentle touch.

He shook away the preposterous notion, as well as the desire, and concentrated instead on what Lissa had just told him. Yet, he needed more information than that. Much more.

"How did Benavides notice you in the first place?"

She hesitated as a sad smile touched her lips. "You know, the funny thing is, this whole situation could've been avoided had my family remained in Gelderland. But my father believed he could provide a better life for his family in the new world. His brother, already established in Sint-Kruis, invited my father several times to join him on the island and become his partner in the merchant trade. So, a few years ago, after my mother's death had taken its toll, he finally accepted the offer.

"Armando Manera still has family ties on the island; he is connected to the natives by blood. So he visits quite often. On one of his visits he presented a favored niece with a beautiful *peineta* for her hair. In Maria's innocent delight, she told him she already knew about the gift, that I had described it in a game we played. When he wheedled the child for more information, she added that I, as well as my sister, could do a lot of things other people couldn't do. That we knew things before they happened.

"He had my sister and me watched, and over time, he gathered sufficient evidence. He then presented all he had learned to Benavides. In turn, they devised their plot. Or, so he claimed."

"Why didn't they take your sister aboard the galleon as well?"

"Margaretha doesn't have the same ability I have, or to the degree I have it. She can heal using medicinal plants well enough, and the things she conjures are more than adequate. But for her, visions are an uncommon occurrence. Since Armando's ruffians never witnessed her having very many, well—" She shrugged away the remainder of her statement.

"So Manera wanted you because he doesn't believe your sister has the ability to see the future as well as you do."

Lissa nodded. "So he could lure me away and set his trap, he kidnapped my sister. Right now she is imprisoned within the citadel in San Juan, Puerto Rico. They've not released her for fear of the repercussions from her abduction. However, so they can justify her imprisonment, the heartless dogs have considered handing her over to the Grand Inquisitor in Brazil. As far as I know, they've not yet decided for fear of Dutch reprisal."

"You were never made aware of this scheme in any of your visions?" he asked.

She closed her eyes, and slowly shook her head. "Just bits and pieces that didn't make any sense until after she disappeared. Since this is all my fault, I had no choice but to go after her and when I finally arrived—"

"I will not allow you to accept the blame, Lissa, Manera and Benavides must take full responsibility for their reprehensible actions, not you. You are as innocent as is your sister."

She sniffed, picked up the cloth, and swirled it around inside the pot.

"Do you know if they made anyone else privy to their plans?"

"I saw two others in vision. One, I think is a guard or is acting as guard. I'm not sure who the other is or what his part in all of this is, though most assuredly, I will recognize his face the moment I see it."

"Exactly where were you when they captured you?"

Lissa replaced the dressing. "In San Juan and within a stone's throw of the fortress that holds my sister. Apparently, a couple of his hired ruffians spied me. Those vile men discovered my presence just as I had immersed myself deep in concentration to draw away the guards. At such a time, I'm unaware of my physical surroundings and somehow, I think they understood that. Now that I'm free of Manera, I must go back before it's too late—"

"That milk-livered scut…" Wolf lifted his head for a moment and winced. He gazed at Lissabeth, as he took a couple deep breaths. "If Rand doesn't have the opportunity to retrieve your sister then I promise you, I will."

Rand huffed out an irritated breath. "Don't be daft, man. Of course I'll fetch her sister. At the same time, we'll ensure that Manera will never again have the opportunity to threaten or harm Lissa. I should've thrown the miserable miscreant into the sea when I had the chance," he muttered.

"Nay, drowning is too easy a death… for what he did… to Lissa," Wolf mumbled. "You… were right about that. We'll help Lissa first. Afterward, we'll take care of Manera in our own way."

Lissa's incredulous gaze darted between both men. "You'd take me back to San Juan?"

"Without a moment's hesitation, and with or without your consent," Rand said. "I'll not leave an innocent woman in the hands of the Spaniards."

"I don't know what to say." Lissa released a slow breath. "Thank you, both of you. I know I'm running out of time—"

"No need for thanks," Rand said. "I assure you, it'll be our pleasure."

Wolf turned to his side as he gazed at Rand. "We need to get there before…someone decides to haul Margaretha to Brazil, Rand. We can't let them…put her in the hands of the Grand Inquisitor. She won't survive…"

"You're right. The problem I see is that we'll have at least another four days at sea before we're close enough to San Juan to drop anchor." Rand looked over at Lissa. "Tell me, when a future event you've seen abruptly changes direction, are you made aware of it through another vision?"

"Sometimes," she replied.

"So, if they move your sister, a new vision might tell you that?"

"I fervently hope so."

"Can you give us the details on what the fortress looks like on the inside? If possible, I need the number and location of all entrances, the strength of the guards, as well as the precise locality of your sister. As you can imagine, the Spaniards have never once invited us in to have a look at the place."

"Yes, I can do that much."

"Good enough. The moment we return to the ship I'll draw up a set of plans with you as my guide. From there, we can decide the best way to get inside the structure and retrieve your sister."

Lissa placed a gentle hand on his arm. "Armando will be a factor in all this. Most likely, he'll rush back to Puerto Rico at the first opportunity, if he's not already well on his way. He knows I have no choice but to return for my sister. He'll prepare for that."

"As will I..." Rand's voice trailed off as he considered the truth of his statement. He quite looked forward to having another *chat* with the man. Would that Benavides could be in attendance as well. "Speaking of Manera, what was the purpose of all those bizarre symbols carved onto the door and the ridiculous arrangement of plant matter?"

"To make escape impossible. The symbols and specific vegetation he used are supposed to hold a witch at bay by rendering her powerless." She shrugged her indifference. "At least that's what he said to the man who nailed the door shut."

"Does the notion have any merit?"

A mischievous smile matched the sudden twinkle in her eyes. "None that I know of."

For a minute or two, he drank in her comeliness. "I've seen you do a couple of interesting things, Lissa. If I had not boarded that galleon, could you have— um—found your way out of that room by yourself?"

She gave him a sideways glance. "The greater problem would've come in escaping the ship. I can't walk on water, Rand, nor can I fly with or without a broom. So what good would it have done to escape the room and give them knowledge I would rather they *not* have until I choose?"

He exaggerated the clearing of his throat. "Well, at least we got that much cleared up."

Her smile gave way to quiet laughter, and he basked in the sound of it. Then Joris and Cornelius returned with a bevy of blankets. The rest of their companions followed close behind.

"Hazael will keep first watch with the crew aboard the ship. He decided on this course of action once we told him how admirable of a job Lissa is doing when it comes to Wolf's care." Joris aimed a thumb behind him. "Andries is bringing up the rear."

Cornelius handed Lissa the blanket on top. "What's even better than that is our wondrous cook brings the fixings for dinner."

Rand nodded as he placed a hand over his stomach. "Sounds good, I'm starving."

"Wolf will need soup." Lissa tucked the blanket around him.

"Already planned on it," said Andries as he crowded past the men and hurried toward the fire. "So everyone make way."

"How's Wolf doing?" asked Joris.

Wolf opened his eyes a crack and saluted. "He's doing very well at the moment… thanks for asking. But then thus far… he's had the best of care."

Joris leaned over, patted his shoulder, and winked at Lissa. "You're a lucky, misbegotten dog, Dircksen, and you don't deserve it. But then again, it's good to know we'll not be mourning your death. You had us all worried there for a minute."

"Oh, you needn't worry about Wolf." Lissa dismissed the comment with a wave of her hand. "I do believe he'll be around for a long time. A very long time, indeed."

Chapter Seven

"Did you hear that, Cornelius?" Laurens rubbed a hand against his mouth. No doubt so he could hide his oh-too-obvious grin. "The lady says Wolf will recover just fine. I suppose you better put the man's dagger back where it goes before he returns to his cabin and finds it missing. The results might not be pretty. After all, he's pretty partial to that knife and you know how churlish he can get."

Sniggers and guffaws followed the comment. Cornelius shrugged.

"Then you should return his compass. He favors that as well and I certainly wouldn't want to be the focus of his anger if I were you." His hazel eyes danced with mischief.

Lissa had never seen such fine camaraderie aboard a ship before. From what she'd witnessed during her various voyages, long days at sea and calamities brought out the worst in people. Yet, among this crew, she found just the opposite, and it made her wonder.

"How did you all come together?"

Joris plunked himself down beside her. "As the most amazing, most renowned crew sailing the seas today, you mean?"

"Or ever," Cornelius added.

"Yes. Did you all know each other beforehand? Were you friends?" she asked as the men found a place, settled down and awaited their evening meal.

A delicious, mouth-watering aroma wafted throughout the cave.

Rand shook his head. "Nay, we all met at various times and places over the course of about three years or so. In regard to the crew? I wanted only the best aboard the *Rood Draeck*. So while the shipwrights labored over her design and construction, I took time and great care in the selection of my men. I believe I did a most excellent job of it too."

"When did you start looking for them?" asked Lissa.

"The moment Hoogteeling put me at the helm of my first merchant ship in the year 1615. I knew then and there I'd have a ship of my own. At that time I discovered Wolf on his first crossing as naught but a passenger from the Duchy of Guelders. The young pup reminded me of myself at that age, so I found I could do naught but take him under my wing. Over the years, I've taught him everything he knows."

Wolf managed a feeble chuckle. "May I remind you, the *young pup* isn't that far behind you in age, Rand?"

"Aye, but you're *years* behind in experience—and in more ways than one, I might add." He winked. After the second round of laughter died down, Rand dipped his head toward Joris. "Now, Wolf and I found young Hoochlandt inside a tavern in New Amsterdam. As I recall, we entered that fine establishment at the tail end of a brawl. Other than those minding their own business, we didn't see another soul standing but him. We asked him what caused all the trouble. He pointed out the largest man in the group. With a look of disdain he said the scoundrel, alongside his honorable, *upstanding* companions, didn't think they should pay his father for the excellent food and service he provided them. Joris thought otherwise and in his own way, told them so."

Lissa gazed at Joris as her mouth dropped. "Really? You stood up to them all by yourself, just like that?"

Joris huffed out a breath. "I gave them ample time to pay."

"So the story goes," said Rand. "Anyway, impressed with his, ah, unique set of skills as well as his attitude, we asked him if he'd rather join us at sea than face the consequences of his actions. One of the men writhing on the floor was the son of the West Indies director. Anyway, in the very moment we made the offer, his father begged us to take him off his hands. Said he was naught but a troublemaker, as I recall."

"As *I* recall the incident," Joris cut in. "You begged my father to let *me* go with *you*."

Rand merely shrugged. "Either way, here you are."

"What about Andries?" asked Lissa, recalling the conversation she had with the cook the morning after her arrival.

Rand's grin broadened. "I stole him from my father."

"We appreciate that, Rand," said Cornelius. "Far more than you know. I mean, I've sailed on ships where the food could kill a man just as quickly and easily as any one of his enemies."

"Aye," Rand agreed. "But Andries is far more than an excellent cook. The man knows the workings of the ship inside and out. At a moment's notice he can take any position I might give him and handle it with astounding expertise. But above all else, from the day of my birth, he has watched my back with the same care he gives his own."

"Well, someone has to watch it," Andries groused, "since you're so careless with it yourself. One might believe you consider yourself immortal for the foolhardy stunts you pull."

Lissa mulled over the troublesome comment as she removed the cloth from Wolf's arm and tossed it back into her pot of water.

That Rand took reckless chances bothered her far more than she cared to admit. She wouldn't allow him—or any member of his crew for that matter—to risk his life to save her sister. If necessary, she'd find a way to go on alone. Lissa caught Rand's questioning gaze and sought a diversion.

"How did you join the crew, Laurens?" she asked.

"I worked on the *kapitein*'s ship during its construction," he replied. "He visited the shipyard on a regular basis as he checked our progress. You see, he designed some unique modifications for the *Rood Draeck* that took a bit of innovation on our part to accomplish. Anyway, throughout it all, we got to know each other fairly well."

Rand nodded. "Laurens amazed me not only with his knowledge of ships, but with the care and attention he gave the detail of each intricate part. Small details that others in his profession simply disregarded or overlooked. He also had some revolutionary ideas that would make for much better and faster sailing. Therefore, upon completion of my vessel I offered him the position of ship's carpenter and he accepted."

Laurens waved off the compliment. "The man pays well."

"Stew's ready," Andries called out amidst the jovial chatter that followed the nonchalant statement. "Help yourself, there's plenty of it."

Rand rose first with the others close at his heels. He grabbed a wooden bowl and filled it to the top with beef stew, thick with potatoes and carrots. He then handed it to her, along with a spoon. She smiled her thanks.

Andries presented Wolf with his soup. In her opinion, the potage smelled just as good as the stew. Yet, Rand's first mate didn't seem all that impressed.

"Not even so much as a small, dried-out biscuit with it?" Wolf inched himself into a more seated position and took the mug.

"Not unless you want to throw it all back up," she said. "I shouldn't think that would be a very pleasant thing for any of us in such close quarters."

Johannes raked his fingers though his auburn hair. He drew his brows together and blew out a breath. "Be grateful you're still alive, and just eat the soup, man. We don't want to sleep outside with the rain pouring down on our heads just because you befouled the place."

"Easy for you to say, Tricault," Wolf muttered. "You're not the one eating it."

"What about you, Johannes? How did you find your way onto the *Draeck*?" Lissa asked.

A far-way look entered his eyes. "A few years ago, Rand spied a galleon heading for Spain. The Spaniards had the ship laden with treasure Rand didn't think they deserved. So he overtook the cumbersome vessel. Once aboard, he found not only the gold and silver, he also found us."

"Us?"

Johannes gazed at Pieter and then aimed a thumb at Conrad Shaers. "About a year prior to Rand's rescue, Conrad, Pieter, and I, along with several other Dutch mariners—who'd been imprisoned by the Spanish— were rounded up and taken aboard the galleon. They used us for slave labor in whatever post they saw fit."

"Aye," said Conrad. "They allowed us very little sleep during our captivity, and what little food they did serve us wasn't fit for dogs. Many times we went without water."

"Yet they were very liberal with the lash," Pieter added.

Rand chuckled. "I'd say you meted out a fair amount of justice, though. Wouldn't you?"

"How so?" Lissa set her empty bowl off to the side.

"The moment we vacated the galleon and returned to my ship, Johannes rushed over to the guns and took control. For the look in his eyes, everyone got out of his way, too. Without a second thought, he blew a hole in the Spaniards' hull that touched off their powder magazine in the process, and all in about two minutes time," Rand said. "Without a shred of remorse, he sent that ship and all her hands straight to the gates of Hell. Pieter and Conrad, a split second behind him, guaranteed the journey. I asked him then if he made that shot on purpose. He turned toward me. With a look of deadly calm, he gave me a curt nod, and simply said, "Aye, *Kapitein*." I appointed Johannes as master gunner on the spot with Pieter and Conrad serving alongside him as gunner's mates. I've never regretted that decision either. They're the finest gunners sailing the seas today."

Lissa lifted her brows. "I see."

Once the discussion of the recollected memory ran its course, her gaze drifted toward Cornelius Arians. After learning about Johannes and his fearless gunners, she didn't know if she should even ask how Rand found his bos'n.

Nonetheless, Rand noted the direction of her gaze. "The day we presented the West Indies Company with the treasure we just talked about, I crossed paths with Cornelius while he served as bos'n aboard the *Dolphijn*. With such an outstanding reputation following him, I asked him if he'd rather sail with us."

Cornelius tossed her a lop-sided grin and nodded. "And indeed I did. I don't know a sailor out there who wouldn't jump at the chance to sail with *Kapitein* Van Locken and the *Rood Draeck*. He and his men are legendary. Once he made the offer, I collected my things and boarded his ship that very day. After all, I didn't want him to change his mind."

Lissa pondered all of their stories as she tended Wolf's injury. Learning a little more about each of them boosted her confidence in their ability. It seemed they could rescue her sister without too much trouble, or so she hoped. She turned toward Hendrick. "Well, I guess that leaves just you."

Amidst the quiet chuckles, Hendrick dropped his gaze to the ground and kicked at a pebble with the toe of his boot. "There's really not that much to tell. I'm not like the others."

"Depending on who you ask," Joris quipped. "Without giving away any of the sordid details, I'll just tell you that Hendrick—alongside Antonis—got into a bit more trouble than what they could get themselves out of. As a result of that trouble, their penurious master doubled the terms of their indenture by adding an additional five years to the terms of their service."

Lissa gazed at Hendrick. "Did you know Antonis before your indenture?"

Hendrick nodded. "He's my cousin."

"He is? I didn't know that," she said.

"You would've seen it in time, I assure you. They have the same, uh, *disposition*, if you get my meaning," said Joris. "Anyway, Rand liked their spunk and ingenuity. He paid their debt on the spot and then invited them aboard the *Draeck* as part of our crew. In turn, they've both become very valuable members."

Lissa found much to admire in *Kapitein* Rand Van Locken and his entire crew. Still, she had one more question of no real consequence. Even so, she wanted an answer. She turned toward him.

"You said you personally designed your ship and had it built to your specifications?"

"Aye."

"Why did you call her the *Rood Draeck*?"

A devilish grin emerged and surprisingly left her a little breathless.

"My mother is Welsh. Just how she ended up in Holland is an interesting story for another time. Because of that Welsh blood she entertained me with stories of her culture when I was but a lad. One of those stories concerned Vortigern's encounter with Merlin when the famous magician was still wet behind the ears. Merlin prophesied that in time, the famous red dragon of Wales would defeat the invading white dragon from Saxony and indeed the creature did, is this not so? Therefore, I thought it fitting to invite the valiant, conquering dragon aboard my vessel by name and at the same time, honor my mother's heritage."

****

Long after Rand's men drifted toward sleep, Lissa stayed awake and tended Wolf's wound. His first mate breathed easy now, and almost all signs of his earlier pain had fled. In all his days he'd never seen the victim of a stingray barb shake off the poison in a matter of hours.

For a while, neither of them said a word. He just watched. All the while her mere presence stirred feelings he'd never experienced with any other woman. Until he discovered Lissa inside that filthy, makeshift prison berth, women were naught but an agreeable diversion who provided pleasant conversation and the like. He didn't want any more from them than that. But now, he didn't know what he wanted. He didn't know if he should embrace these strange feelings, or back away from them—and her—altogether.

The longer he thought on it, the more absurd the notion of withdrawing from the girl seemed. He spewed out a breath of laughter. How could he possibly avoid her when she roamed freely about his ship? Especially when he held no will or desire to steer clear of the intriguing woman?

"What's so funny?" she asked quietly.

"Just all of this," he said, making his answer as vague as he could get it.

She wrung out the cloth and instead of putting it back into her pot, she placed it near the fire where it could dry.

"By all of this you mean the dilemma I've involved all of you in?"

"I wouldn't call it a dilemma," he said as he looked at her crystal. "More like waking from an impossible dream only to find you didn't dream at all."

"I'm so sorry. I didn't mean to cause you such anxiety." She dropped her talisman inside her bodice.

"You didn't, and you needn't be sorry. I'd not have my present situation any different than what it is right now." He pointed at her hidden pendant. "How did you come by that thing, anyway?"

"My talisman?" She glanced down at the piece and shrugged. "We simply found each other."

"You *found* each other?"

A touch of humor lit up her beautiful eyes. "Is that so hard for you to believe?"

"What? After everything else you told me earlier? Why would you think something like that?" He fought a grin that threatened escape but lost the battle. "So you found each other then. Just how did that happen?"

"Well, on a rainy spring morning while in my twelfth year, I awoke and heard the crystal calling me. For several miles I followed her enchanting song along the twists and turns of the river. Then, as I waded into the rippling water, I spied a luminous glow emanating from deep within the riverbank. From there, I simply picked up the stone."

"Now why doesn't that surprise me," he muttered.

Soft laughter followed his comment. "Didn't you know? Every descendant of the *Witte Wieven* finds her amulet in such a way. Mine just happened to be waiting for me in the muddy banks of the river near my home in Eefde. Stories such as mine are probably why people think we're Elves."

"No doubt. But, what if someone else had found it first?" he asked. "Would it perform for them as it performs for you?"

"Our talismans appear as nothing more than common rock while they're buried in the earth, or under a tree root, body of water, or wherever. No one would even pick them up, much less covet them. The same doesn't hold true after we take possession of them, though. Although talismans have been stolen many times before, the thief soon discovers he's taken naught but a dull, useless stone. Once he finds it has no value, he'll toss it by the wayside soon enough."

"In such cases, does the talisman ever find its way back to its proper owner?"

"Always."

The declaration gave rise to another thought. "Why didn't Manera take yours away from you?"

"He never saw it. I wore a cloak at the time of my capture and therefore I hid it away before he relieved me of my herbs and what little wardrobe I carried with me."

Rand pondered her words as he watched the flame, built, he supposed, using the power of her crystal. All of it—her entire explanation—seemed beyond the bounds of all possibility or reason. He would've dismissed it as absurd if not for what he'd witnessed with his own eyes. Then he remembered something else someone once said about the *Witte Wieven* that seemed just as absurd.

"You're not immortal, are you?"

Lissa laughed outright. "I wondered if you'd get around to that question. The simple answer is no. We have the same life spans as everyone else, the same human frailties as everyone else. That's why I'm so very worried about Margaretha. There's nothing inside that tiny room she can use that will ward off illness or disease. Should the Spaniards dare haul her before the Inquisition those in authority would convict her of witchcraft. Soon thereafter, they would tie her to a wooden post. The council would then light a fire beneath her feet, and she would die. There's nothing she could do that would stop her death."

"In the same situation, would you? Being tied to the stake under threat of fire, I mean."

Her gaze never left his. "I honestly don't know. I suppose it would depend on the elements around me."

Well, he did know one thing in this moment, and he knew it with absolute certainty. No one would ever get close enough to Lissa to test the notion, whether she had the proper elements or not. In light of that, he and his men would plan the rescue of her sister with more care than he'd ever given anything else before.

"Earlier this evening you said the Spaniards delayed their decision concerning Margaretha, for fear of Dutch reprisal. Now, don't get me wrong, I know how important your sister is to you and to your entire family. Yet, as a general rule in a matter such as this, your Dutch governor wouldn't send a force in numbers the Spaniards would fear, if they even sent anyone at all. I'm sure you know this. So what did you mean by the remark?"

Lissa didn't answer right away. Instead, she inspected the cloth, and finding it dry, she gently wrapped it around Wolf's injury. Once she tied it off, she covered him with his blanket and then brushed her hand against his forehead.

"Lissa?"

Finally, she looked up and met his gaze. "You've never asked me for my surname, Rand."

"Nay, I guess I haven't given it a second thought, at least I didn't until you brought it to my attention. I'm sorry for the oversight. Despite my tardiness, would you introduce yourself fully to me now?" he asked.

She took in a deep breath. "My name is Lissabeth Capoen. I am the daughter of Arjaen Capoen and the niece of—"

"Frans Capoen," he finished for her. "The Governor of Sint-Kruis Island."

She nodded. A thousand different thoughts bombarded his mind.

"They don't know about any of this, do they. Your father and uncle, I mean."

"No, they don't. At least, not yet. Right now all they know is that three men took my sister against her will. The witnesses didn't have any more information than that. My uncle is of a mind to believe the English—with whom they have an ongoing quarrel—or perhaps even the island natives are holding her for ransom. He has men looking for her, as we speak."

"Why didn't you tell them the Spaniards took her to Puerto Rico?"

"When my father asked, I didn't know. By the time I had my first vision of her sitting inside her prison room, he and the search party had already gone."

"So, he doesn't know you left the island yourself, then."

"No, and with a bit of luck, he won't find out. Before I left on this journey, I told various family members as well as a few neighbors that I didn't feel safe in our home. I'd decided to stay with friends for a while and to let my father know should he return before me. If that should happen then I'm sure my father will believe I made the right choice. He won't even question it. While he's busy looking for Margaretha, he won't worry about me."

"Yet, should either your father or your uncle somehow discover the malicious details which Benavides and Manera concocted, your notoriously temperamental uncle will indeed rally the Dutch forces. A full scale war between the Spaniards and the Dutch could possibly follow such an act. So, you're right. The Spaniards would both know and fear this possibility."

"The thing is, I haven't seen any such occurrence in any of my visions. Therefore, I must believe, or at least hope, I can handle this situation myself."

"Not without our help, you won't. I won't allow it."

She lowered her gaze, rubbed her hands back and forth against her palms, and nodded. "Thank you. I appreciate all the help I can get."

"Have you seen anything else concerning the matter?"

"Not yet, and there's no guarantee I will either, Rand." She paused. "We just might find ourselves walking into something far bigger than what either of us is prepared to handle."

"Not so. My men and I always plan for the worst possibility in situations such as this and then hope like crazy it doesn't happen. Because of that, we're well prepared, trust me. Besides, with such a lovely lady witch at our side, how could we possibly fail to complete our task?" he teased in an effort to lighten her mood.

A slight smile touched her lips, yet she said nothing in response. The haunted look in her eyes gripped his heart with a ferocity that surprised him. He brushed her hair away from her face and then caressed the length of her jaw. At once she drew in a shallow breath and for a moment, she held onto it.

"Don't worry, Lissa," he whispered. "I won't let anything happen to your sister or to you."

She gulped. "Right now, I'm not as worried about me as I am of you and your crew. I would never forgive myself if something terrible befell you or anyone else aboard your ship because you helped me free my sister."

"Nothing will happen to any of us, I give you my solemn vow."

She closed her eyes. "People say that so easily. Yet, more often than not, vows are far easier to break than they are to keep."

He shook his head. "Not mine and not this time."

Chapter Eight

The gentle roll of thunder and patter of rain gave Lissa little incentive to rise. But most of Rand's crewman had already abandoned their blankets and busied themselves with various chores even as the storm continued its assault on the island. Even though she'd rather stay snuggled in her covers, she supposed she should rise as well. After all, despite his vast improvement, Wolf still needed attention and care. She smothered a yawn, tossed her blankets off to the side, and sat up.

"Ah, our lovely lady is awake," said Joris.

"So she is." Andries grinned as he dished up her breakfast. "I hope you're hungry."

She accepted the bowl of what he called his "famous island porridge" and smiled. "I am. Thank you."

"I imagine Wolf still gets just the broth?" he asked.

"Yes, I'm afraid so, at least for the remainder of the day. Come tomorrow he'll be strong enough to eat something a little more substantial."

Rand chuckled as he settled himself down beside her. He glanced over at Wolf. "Another day? He won't like that much, so prepare yourself for all of his complaints. He's not a man that likes to skimp on meals as you've probably already noted."

She met the captain's mirthful gaze and shrugged.

"Complaints notwithstanding, he must endure the soup or suffer the consequences. Believe me, he'd rather not face the alternative of what eating a full breakfast would provoke inside his belly."

Though Wolf hadn't opened his eyes, he expelled an exasperated breath. "You're a merciless, hard-hearted woman, Lissa. Do you know that?"

"Only when I tend the sick and afflicted, and do what's best for them," she countered.

"Must be a trait of the *Witte Wieven*," said Joris. "I've always heard they were a daunting bunch of women."

"And must be avoided at all cost," Laurens added.

Lissa breathed out a laugh and shook her head. She found it obvious from their comments that while she slept, Rand had shared the details of her life and circumstances with his crewmen. If their lighthearted banter and smiles were any indication, the full knowledge of her background and her purpose didn't faze them in the least.

"Oh, come on now, we're not all that bad," she said.

"Are you kidding me?" Hendrick assumed a horrified expression as he clutched at his heart. "Everyone knows that when the eerie mists rise up from the grave hills, the ghost-witches are out and about. I've heard it said that during such an event, one should head straight home, slam the door behind him, and lock the place up tight. Cowering underneath the covers isn't a bad thing to do either."

"Aye, that's exactly what I've heard as well, and with nary dilly-dallying along the way," Cornelius chimed in. "By all accounts, the witches are looking for victims to satisfy their blood-lust, mayhap a baby to steal, or even a hapless man to violate."

"Do they really?" asked Johannes amidst the boisterous laughter that filled the cave. "Well, if Lissa is one of them, then I'll step forward and courageously volunteer for the latter duty. That way the rest of you can rest easy."

"Oh, I just bet you would," said Pieter. "The truth of the matter is that she probably wouldn't give you so much as a second glance. Not while I'm standing in the same line anyway. And as much as it might hurt, you know I speak the truth."

"Dreamers, the both of you," muttered Conrad as he waved a hand in dismissal. "But tell me something Lissa; is there any truth at all in the ghostly legends concerning the Wise Women? I only ask because all the days of her life, my mother swore that as a young girl she saw one while living in Zwiep in the Achterhoek. She's not the only one that stands as witness either. Now, keep in mind the people in her village both respect and revere these enchanting women. Encountering one is something that is desirable and should be bragged about. Now having said that, I've always believed, that because of this high regard, they saw what they wanted to see in the mists. I mean, ghosts don't really exist, do they?"

Lissa dabbed at the corners of her mouth as she glanced at Rand. He seemed truly interested in her response. But then, so did everyone else. Her gaze fell on Conrad as she shrugged.

"If you're asking whether or not some of my ancestors lingered after their death, then the answer is yes. Some of them, by choice, have remained behind in their spiritual state, as do other spirits of men and women born to this earth. Whether you believe it or not, they aren't figments of the imagination, nor do all have a desire to spread fear or ill will."

"You're serious about that, aren't you?" said Joris.

She nodded. "Yes, I am. What's more, I can assure you the souls of the *Wieven* don't steal babies, kill innocent people, or carry bloody whips and handkerchiefs as proof of their heinous deeds. These women spent their entire mortal lives helping people. The need and disposition for such, doesn't change after their deaths. Rather, those who've remained behind feel they can be of greater service to the living than they can in the world of spirits. In my opinion, it's a very charitable thing for them to do."

"I wonder why, then, so many people actually fear the *Wieven* and believe the worst," said Cornelius.

Lissa let go of a heavy sigh. She gazed toward the entrance of the cave without really seeing it. "The falsehoods began centuries ago with a few overzealous ministers who demonized everything they didn't understand. This included the *Witte Wieven*. They denounced the skill and knowledge of my ancestors as pagan in nature and born of evil. I'd also assume part of it comes as a direct result of those who begged the assistance of the deceased women and have done so without thought to the consequences of their requests. Many times the outcome is not what they had envisioned or desired. In return for their displeasure, they tarnish the reputation of the one person who deigned to help them in the best manner she saw fit."

"I can see where something like that might happen," said Joris as his gaze took in each of his mates. "Think of all the outright lies you hear concerning Rand and the *Draeck*. Every last one of them originates from our enemies or those who are envious of his many, notable accomplishments."

"That they do," said Andries as he handed Wolf a mug filled with hot, steaming broth, which he grudgingly accepted. "Those stories have circulated ever since they made Rand a captain when but a lad. I remember shortly after the announcement, a very large assemblage of seamen cast lots over how long they thought it would take for him to sink a ship. As I recall, most of them wagered it would be on his very first crossing."

"Did they now?" said Rand.

Andries nodded as he chuckled. "Aye, and as the fates would have it, I ran into the lout that started it all last time we made port in Amsterdam. I asked him if anyone still had charge over that dusty old pot of his and if so, what they planned on doing with it after all this time."

"What did he say for himself?" asked Laurens.

"Not much he could say," Andries replied. "He simply muttered something about the foolishness of youth and walked away."

The crewmen roared with laughter and at once defended their captain as only they could. Rand grinned and shook his head while a barrage of barbs and insults—directed toward those who took part in the wager—filled the cave.

As the hilarity died down, Joris turned toward Andries. "Give me a list of their names, so I can hunt them down and squash them like the insects they are. Shouldn't take me all that long, all things considered."

The comment set off another round of boisterous chatter concerning various imaginable ways they could afflict their unseen enemies.

"All right, that's enough of that now," said Rand, taking command of the situation. "Since the rain is naught but a drizzle, let's take advantage. I want all of you to go out and fetch the water barrels. See they're filled and take them back to the ship. Now is also a good time to replenish our food stock. So get on out there and do a little hunting or catch some fish."

As the men set off, Lissa knelt down beside Wolf. She put a gentle hand on his forehead and then moved it down his cheek. "How are you feeling today, Wolf?"

"As fit as a fiddle. I can leave my sick bed with ease if everyone would just get out of my way and let me do it," he replied.

"I'm happy you feel that way. Truly, I am. Nonetheless, your body took a very harsh blow yesterday. I'm not sure you appreciate just how sick you were. Nonetheless, in order for you to heal properly, you need a lot of rest."

Wolf shook his head and *tsk*ed. "All of this resting on my backside is making me a loon. I don't know if I can endure another—"

"You can, and you will and that, my friend, is a direct order," said Rand. "We don't need you having a relapse when a couple of very special ladies need our help in the immediate future."

Lissa met the captain's gaze and smiled. The wink he returned disturbed the nest of butterflies that had somehow invaded her stomach the moment her gaze first fell on Rand Van Locken. A vexing blush appeared on her cheeks from the tumult.

"I won't quibble over that," said Wolf as he propped himself up on his elbow. "While we're on the subject of that particular bit of business, I've a question that has plagued my mind."

"Ask away," she said, grateful for any excuse to move her past the discomfort.

"How often do you have these visions of yours?" he asked.

She tilted her head. "There's no set pattern, really. I can have several of them within the span of just a few days. Then again, there've been times I've gone several weeks without having any at all."

"Do you ever find them meaningless?" Wolf asked.

She drew her brows together. "Meaningless?"

"What I mean is, a vision of no real importance, one that's just a glimpse into someone's future that might not concern you at all. Something like a party someone is planning or a mundane daily duty of some kind."

"Sometimes they begin that way," she said as the vision concerning Wolf crashed into her mind. "But throughout my life I've learned they always connect to something far more important—something vital to me or to the person I see in vision. Sometimes, the connection takes a very long time to manifest itself. For this reason, I always pay close attention to them when they come."

Rand considered her explanation far longer than she believed he would. Where had his thoughts taken him?

"From what you've told me then, Armando Manera doesn't understand you cannot have a vision at will," he said.

Lissa nodded. "That's right, he doesn't. Like most people, he thinks we can just look into someone's eyes, or like the gypsies, take someone's hand and see the future. This is the very falsehood he'll present to the king of Spain. The king will believe him."

"The man's an idiot. Such a thing could cost you your life if you don't deliver the visions the king demands," Rand said.

"I know."

****

Those two words, softly spoken, haunted Rand throughout the remainder of the day. Countless times he envisioned the forms of torture the king of Spain would foist upon Lissa if she didn't give him what he demanded. She would fail too, regardless of the agony she'd endure. Even if she made something up, the falsehood would soon reveal itself. Had he but known Armando's intentions, he wouldn't have been so lenient with the man when he first crossed his path. When next they met, and they would meet, he'd correct the oversight.

"What has you so deep in thought?"

Rand turned his head. Lissa stood just beside him at the entrance of the cave. The storm had abated, and the brilliance of the stars illuminated her lovely face. So much so, he saw her willow-green eyes searching his without need of additional light. Did she see or even sense the inner rage he now directed at Manera? He hoped not. At once, he looked up at the heavens, took in a breath and slowly released it. Then, with his emotions under firm control, he gazed at her again and offered a smile.

"What am I thinking? Why, nothing more than

your incredible ability to heal," he said. "As well as how very grateful I am you were here and saved Wolf's life."

She looked at him askance. "Is that all?"

"Does that surprise you?"

"Well, no, I suppose not. It's just that you looked so—" She stopped short and drew her brows together.

"Wolf is a very good friend, Lissa. I wouldn't have wanted death to claim him in the prime of his life."

"Death wouldn't even have had the chance, if not for me," she whispered.

"You take too much on yourself, Lissa. You take responsibility for things which are not your fault or for which you have no control over." He shrugged. "Who knows but that you might've saved all of our lives when fate stepped in and arranged our unexpected meeting? Did you ever stop to consider that?"

Soft laughter escaped her lips. "Now, how could I have possibly accomplished such a wondrous thing?"

"Oh, I don't know. If we hadn't encountered the galleon, we would've assisted Heyn as ordered. At the end of whatever might've taken place that dawn, we would've sailed on to wherever the winds took us. Mayhap in so doing, we might've encountered an enemy ship and engaged her in battle. In turn, that ship could very well have sent the *Rood Draeck* and all her hands to the bottom of the sea. Should that have happened, then at this very moment we would be naught but food for your mermaids."

She shivered even as her eyes filled with something he couldn't quite name. At once she lowered her gaze and gulped. When she looked at him again, she did naught but smile. Yet, the look in her eyes didn't at all match the expression on her face. Why? Where had her thoughts taken her?

She shook her head. "Not from what I hear. Your crewmen are all in awe of the way you take on your enemies and then sail away unscathed."

"You mustn't take everything they say to heart. They all exaggerate to the point of embarrassment," he said.

The bantered comment, meant to tease, erased the smile from her face. He silently berated himself as he held a hand toward her and cocked his head toward the windswept trees.

"You know, I'm sure that breeze would do you a world of wonders after being cooped up for the last couple of days. Let's escape the cave for a while and take a little stroll. How does that sound?"

She didn't answer. Instead, she glanced at the inner chamber as she bit down on her lip.

"I promise we won't go far. If someone needs us, for any reason whatsoever, all they need do is call out and we would hear them," he said.

Her smile returned as she accepted his hand. "You know what? A walk with you sounds heavenly."

For a while neither of them said anything as they headed seaward. Just as he hoped, he didn't see worry or concern in her eyes. As they made a pathway through the palm trees, she turned her gaze toward the ocean. They couldn't see it yet, but the intensity of the salty brine and the crash of the waves against the shore stated they were close. She took in a deep breath, slowly released it, and then nodded.

"This is exactly what I need right now," she murmured. "Thank you, Rand."

"There's no need for thanks," he said. "In my mind, you're the one who did me the favor by accompanying me."

"Is that so? Well, I want to thank you, nonetheless."

He pressed her hand a little before relinquishing it. "So, even after living most of your life in Eefde, it seems you've developed a liking for the sea. Am I right?"

"Oh, I love the ocean. The need to develop it didn't exist because I fell in love with its magnificence the moment I saw it. The smell, the roar and the power of the waves—be they gentle or fierce—just everything about it touches my soul."

Rand chuckled. "Lissa, you're a woman after my own heart."

She responded with a soft breath of laughter and shook her head. "The love of the ocean didn't come readily to Margaretha though. She was so seasick at first. Yet, by the time we reached Sint-Kruis, her attitude had changed a bit. Ever since our arrival on the island, we've taken morning walks along the beach. We'll collect shells and whatnot and all at her insistence. Well, at least we did."

"She adjusted well to life on the island then?" he asked.

"Oh, I don't know. I think if one asked her preference, she would probably just as soon go home. After what's happened to her since our arrival, perhaps that might be the best thing for her, after all."

"Do you think your father would let her return if given the chance?" he asked. "Perhaps let her take up residence with one of your sisters?"

"I suppose that's possible. There are times I've wondered if even he regrets his decision to leave our village. My father is, or at least he was, a farmer by trade. Although the farm never made him a rich man, we always had enough food on our table and plenty we could share with those who needed it." She shrugged. "At times I look at his face though, and I see a longing in his eyes. I don't know if he simply misses my mother, my sisters, or if it's his life in Eefde he longs for. Yet, after he booked our passage—and more times than I can count—he said he couldn't turn back on the decision made. Did he say that because he didn't think he could go home? Or, did he say it because he's determined to make a new life here, whatever the personal cost?"

"That's a question only he can answer. Once we free Margaretha from the vile hands of the Spanish, I vow I'll give him the chance to answer it," he said. "How would you like that?"

"The chance? What do you mean?"

"I mean that should he wish to return to your village, I'll personally make sure he gets there." The spontaneous offer surprised him. Why on earth did he simply assume Lissa would be a permanent resident aboard his ship?

Her mouth dropped and she gazed upon him as if he'd taken leave of his senses. He barely held back his laughter.

"You would take us all the way to Eefde?"

He paused as her words hit home. Despite that fact, he nodded.

"Why would you do that when you have other more pressing things to do? You made a commitment to the West India Company, so—"

"You saved Wolf's life, Lissa. Taking your family home is the least I can do, should that be the choice your father makes."

"You don't think risking your life while rescuing Margaretha is payment enough?"

"Nay. The retrieval of your sister won't take us more than a week or two at most, and that includes the journey to San Juan and back to Sint-Kruis," he said. "The way I look at it, Wolf's life is far more valuable than a couple weeks of our time."

"That's very kind of you, Rand, and, I appreciate the offer," she said. "Truly, I do. But, there's just no way I could allow you—"

"I'm not asking. Despite any objections you might have, I'll discuss the matter with your father. The only question you need answer right now, is whether or not you think he'll take me up on the offer?" He lifted a brow and grinned. "I only ask so I know how to plan for the immediate future. Unless of course, you've already seen such a voyage in vision and can just tell me."

She shook her head and laughed. "I haven't seen anything that would indicate such a journey. At least, not yet. Therefore, I guess we'll both just have to wait and see how it all turns out."

Chapter Nine

Lissa rose early and tiptoed around the handful of sleeping men that had remained on the island for the second night in a row despite the storm. A warm, cloudless sky greeted the rising of the sun and she welcomed it with arms wide open. She stepped out of the cave and weaved through the tangle of trees intent on a much-needed bath. The Spaniards had never offered her one nor would she have accepted the offer even if the degenerates had.

She removed all of her dirty, tattered clothing, save her chemise, and waded into the gentle flow of the water. Layers of dirt covered her ragged skirt, petticoat and bodice. Without soap she couldn't possibly purge all of the stains from the cloth. Still, she cleaned the soil as best she could by rubbing the fabric together and letting the water currents do the rest. After she finished the chore, she hung them on a tree branch to dry. Once again, she immersed herself in the clear, blue river. She dallied far longer than she had planned for the simple joy of the swim that followed her bath. But finally, with a bit of reluctance, she swam toward the riverbank and climbed out.

Just as her bare feet touched the grass, a warm blanket engulfed her shoulders. She sucked in a breath as she grabbed hold of the generous folds and wrapped them snugly around her body. At once, she whirled around and faced her unknown benefactor.

"I thought you might need a blanket after your early morning swim." A simple, though elegant ensemble was draped over his arm. "I also thought you could use these since you sacrificed your own clothes while tending Wolf."

As her heart returned to its normal rhythm, her hand explored the softness of the fine fabric. "Where did you get them?"

He shrugged away the question. "They've been languishing away on my ship for quite some time now. I had my men retrieve them the other night while they collected the blankets. They're not much, I know, nor are they the latest fashion, I'm sure. However, at least they're still in good repair, and what's more, they're clean and dry."

She smiled as she accepted his gift. "Thank you, Rand. I appreciate your thoughtfulness. Now, if you'll just turn around for a moment, I'll see if they fit."

He turned about and waited as she dressed. "Uh, when I woke up and found you missing, I thought perhaps you'd gone outside to, um, refresh yourself. But when you didn't return in a timely manner, I worried that something might've befallen you. So, I went looking and as it happened, I saw, rather what I mean to say is that by chance I happened to, uh—"

She couldn't help but laugh over the awkward explanation of his presence with blanket and clothing in hand. "You needn't worry, Rand," she said, "I don't think you spied on me from afar."

The captain blew out a relieved breath and nodded as she tied the lovely, emerald-green skirt over the fine, delicate petticoat. As she laced up the matching green bodice over the ruffled white smock, she admired the floral embroidery on the neckline and sleeves. She couldn't help but wonder then to whom the garments once belonged. Of course, one might also ask why the woman didn't take them with her when she vacated the ship.

What the captain does and with whom he does it is not my concern. "You can turn about now if you wish. Lucky for me, they're a perfect fit."

As his gaze meandered over her form, he dipped his head in approval. "That they are. The color suits you as well, Lissa. You look very lovely."

"Thank you."

An unwanted blush stained her cheeks. She combed her fingers through the mass of tangles as she sought a quick change in subject.

"Is Wolf awake yet?"

"Aye. The man woke up famished. He said he feels just fine and demanded something solid for breakfast despite any orders to the contrary from the enchanting woman with an extraordinary ability to heal."

"I'm very happy to hear it. But he needn't concern himself. He can eat anything he wants, when he wants, and as often as he'd like now."

"That's good news for all of us." He paused for a moment. "I take it then we've nothing more to worry about in regard to his recovery? No relapses or after-effects?"

"No, nothing at all, I should think. Still, I'll make him a healing tea this morning anyway, if I can find the makings for it on this island, that is. The tea will make him feel much stronger."

Rand gazed all about their environment. "So, how

do you accomplish that? I mean, do you just walk about and examine the vegetation until you find those mysterious fixings for your tea?"

"Yes, I suppose that about sums it up."

"All right, then. When did you think you'd conduct your search?"

"The sooner the better, but first—" She ripped off a generous piece of cloth from her old petticoat and ripped it in sections along the borders. With a bit of intricate knot work, she fashioned a bag. "There, I think that should do it."

"Are you ready for us to explore the island then?"

Though the offer of his company surprised her, she hoped she didn't show it. "Yes, I am."

He extended an open hand. "Then shall we?"

His fingers closed around hers the moment she placed her hand on top of his. They wandered amid the shrubs, trees and flowers at a leisurely pace. All the while she inspected the green grass, branches as well as the blossoms in vivid shades of pink, yellow and red. Along the way she collected an assortment of stems, leaves, and seeds from the abundant vegetation this heavenly island provided.

"You need all of that for just one mug of tea?" Rand gazed pointedly at her bag that all but spilled over with everything she had gathered.

"No, but since the herbs on the island are plentiful, I thought I'd collect what I could. The herbs will replace what Armando took away from me after my capture. After all, I may need them at some point in time."

"By all the saints, I certainly hope not," he murmured. "We don't need a repeat of what happened to Wolf."

"No, we don't, but it doesn't hurt to be prepared for all kinds of emergencies, does it?"

"I suppose not."

He again took hold of her hand and they resumed their journey. As they followed the turn of the river, she spied a tree that had a smooth, light brown bark, twisting branches and small green, pointed leaves. The aura surrounding it reflected all its colors, outlining it in blue and yellow hues. It was the very thing she needed most, and she tugged him toward it.

"Rand, would you scrape a thin layer of bark from this tree with your knife?" she asked. "I no longer have mine."

"I can see why Manera might take that. Might be dangerous in the hands of an irritated woman." He grinned as he withdrew the dagger from his belt and headed for the flower-laden tree. "Did he take anything else?"

"Except for my crystal, he took everything I had, even what few clothes I carried with me."

"Now, why doesn't that surprise me? Tell me, though, what do you use the bark for?"

"Here on this island, it's one of the greatest ingredients nature provides for fighting infection."

"I see." He gazed at her talisman. "I thought that thing you wear around your neck took care of that the other night. At least, from my point of view it appeared so."

She grasped her pendant and held it up toward the sky. It sparkled like diamonds under the light of the sun. Glorious colors shot out in every direction. "Yes, it did. But the tea will make sure it doesn't return. The pulpy substance extracted from the bark will also heal any other damage his body might've sustained from the venom. For that too, is still a concern."

"I see. So tell me, how does it work?"

"What? The tea?"

He handed her the small handful of collected chips in varying shades of green and brown. "Nay, your crystal."

"Oh, that. Well, it channels the energy from whatever source I choose and then transfers it into my body. I can then use it however I wish."

"The source? I'm not sure I understand what you mean by that."

"The source is nothing more than the natural energy every element gives us. The earth and everything that grows in it, the water and even the very air we breathe, all exude a unique, natural energy. I simply draw that energy into the crystal and take it into myself. From my early childhood I was tutored in the various ways one can build on that energy and use it for the good it can do."

He tilted his head and gave her a sideways glance. "Like spontaneous fire, for instance, when that fire is needed? Or even create a mysterious fog that engulfs a ship and then moves said vessel an incredible distance in a matter of minutes?"

Her expression smacked of guilt. Not only did she sense it from the heated blush that followed, but the humor that filled his eyes provided sufficient evidence as well. She nibbled on a nail. She wouldn't lie, she couldn't.

"Are you angry about that?"

A quiet chuckle followed her question. "Nay, I

can't say that I am. However, I do wonder why you felt the need."

If she told him the truth would he feel even more beholden to her? She didn't want his help out of a sense of duty or obligation. *If such proved the case he'd take foolish chances—*

"Lissa?"

"This is a question that troubles you? One you feel you must have an answer for?"

"Aye, I do. Please don't be afraid of me, Lissa."

She swallowed past the knot in her throat. "I'm not afraid of you. That isn't it at all."

"Is it that you don't trust me then?"

"No, Rand. I trust you with my life. I hope you know that."

At once his eyes filled with both tenderness and warmth. "Then tell me."

"Well, in my first vision I saw Wolf through the haze of gunfire. His was the only face I saw clearly. He spied an enemy ship and yelled out the warning. In response to the warning you told Johannes to man the guns. You…began issuing another command, but you…you couldn't finish it."

He cupped her face and gently wiped away a tear that had fallen aimlessly down her cheek. She hadn't even noticed it. "Here now, we'll have none of that. I'm sure this vision of yours couldn't have been all that bad—"

"Oh, but it was! You couldn't finish the command Rand, because…" She gulped as she placed a trembling hand over her mouth. "Because in that moment you were shot by musket fire. You didn't survive the blow to your heart. A split second after you fell; a cannon ball blew this huge hole in the side of your ship. Many members of your crew died alongside you. Don't you see? I couldn't let any of that happen. I just couldn't. I had to save you! So, I…I stopped the event from taking place in the only way I knew how, even if it meant you believed me the witch Manera accused me of being."

Rand shook his head ever so slightly. He moved a half-step closer. Her feet remained firmly anchored. A magnetic charge—unlike any she'd ever felt before—filled the space between them. Did he feel it too?

His expression softened. Her insides churned. With slow deliberation he brushed his fingers against her cheek and then through the length of her tresses. The beat of her heart accelerated as warmth flowed from head to foot.

All rational thought fled her mind as he tipped her chin upward.

****

A thousand thoughts swirled inside his mind; from the miraculous way she had saved him and his men, to the overwhelming desire to have her in his arms.

"An enchantress you are, my lady, for surely you have bewitched me. You don't know how grateful I am you did that and not just because you saved my life," he whispered.

His hands dropped to the small of her back and then slowly navigated upward. Rand cuddled her so close to his heart he could feel the rapid beat of hers. He leaned close to her lips.

Lissa shivered. Her arms found their way up his chest and around his shoulders. Just as their lips touched, Laurens called Rand's name. He was close by. Too close, in fact. Rand heaved out an irritated sigh, dropped his hands, and backed away. His gaze never once broke away from hers. Neither of them, it seemed, would willingly break the spellbinding connection that joined them together still.

"Aye?" he growled out.

Dead branches and twigs crunched louder until at last, Laurens emerged from the shadows.

"Ah. There you both are. Andries thought something might've befallen your path since you failed to return in what he deemed a sufficient amount of time," he said.

"And just what did he think might've happened to us, Laurens?" Rand ground out.

Laurens shrugged. "Oh, I don't know, he said something about giant sea creatures swallowing you whole. Sharks having you for breakfast and using your bones to pick the hair from their teeth after they finished a most gratifying meal, of course. We found it far easier to search for you than to argue with the man."

"We're standing on dry land, Laurens."

"Aye, we mentioned that as well. Then he went off about sink holes, snakes, poisonous spiders, well, you know how he can get."

Rand drew in a deep breath and blew it out again. "Aye, I know *just* how he can get."

Despite his annoyance, Lissa peeked up at him through lowered lashes and blessed him with a charming smile. In response to that smile, words escaped him. He found he could do naught but claim her hand and head for the cavern. Laurens continued his mindless prattle all the way back, and it grated on his nerves far more than it should have.

Yet, how long would it take before he and Lissa

found the opportunity for another such moment?

"See?" Joris looked up from his seat on the rock and flung a hand toward them the moment they stepped out of the trees. "Just like I told you, they're safe and sound."

Andries merely grunted in response. The men had already vacated the rocky chamber and moved into the sunshine. They chatted amicably amongst themselves. A blazing fire warmed Andries' island porridge. As they joined the crew around the fire, the cook fetched a couple of bowls. He filled them to the top and presented them.

Lissa gave him a sweet smile as they settled down next to Wolf. "Thank you Andries. After I finish my breakfast, would you mind if I share your fire? Wolf needs a special cup of tea."

"Not at all," he replied. "Help yourself."

She shifted her gaze toward Rand's first mate. "How are you feeling today, Wolf?"

"Like the barb from the stingray never happened, and I want to thank you for that. You saved my life, Lissa. You'll ever hold a special place in my heart."

"That's a very kind thing for you to say. But, there's no need for thanks. I'm just happy I could help."

"You did more than help. We both know that. In return, I again vow I'll do all in my power to retrieve your sister," he said. "Anything else you want after that, I'm in your service.

Rand nodded. "That we will. *Both* of us."

"All of us," shouted out his crewmen.

Rand acknowledged his crew with a bow before he turned toward Wolf. "Tell me, Wolf, can you sail, or do you still need more time here on the island?"

"I'm fine. I told you that yesterday as you might recall," he replied.

"Then I think we should hoist anchor and chart a course for San Juan as soon as we resupply the ship," he said.

"Aye, the sooner the better," Wolf replied. "We're wasting precious time on this island."

Rand tossed his empty bowl off to the side and rose to his feet. "All right men let's get ready to sail. If we can collect a bit more fish and fowl before the sun rises much higher, then all the better. If not, we'll go with what we have. It's time for us to quit this place."

As the men fanned out, Lissa took her bag and tossed bits and pieces of her gathered herbs into a cup. Once she made Wolf's tea, he downed it in a single gulp. Rand contemplated the task that awaited them. What they needed most they didn't have. Time. Yet, perhaps they could remedy that and quite possibly even arrive well ahead of Manera.

"Lissa," he said, "You moved my ship quite a distance from Matanzas Bay in just a matter of minutes. The journey to this island should've taken at least two more days with a strong wind as our ally. So—"

"What's this?" asked Wolf and Joris almost in unison.

Rand waved them off. "I'll tell you later. Lissa?"

"You're wondering how close I can get your ship to San Juan and in a relatively short amount of time?" she asked.

"Aye."

"I can help with the distance. This you now know. But the problem is in getting too close. There's always a danger of colliding with another ship coming in or out of the harbor. This isn't something I can see or predict, nor would you want your ship appearing on top of the ocean with a host of witnesses' present. There's one more thing that occurred to me, and you should consider it while making your plans."

"What would that be?"

"By now I'm sure Armando has learned your identity as well as the name of your ship. The crewmen aboard the galleon would've given him that information the moment they freed him from the berth. Therefore, in all likelihood, he and his accomplices will watch the harbor for any sign of the *Draeck* in the event you agreed to rescue my sister."

"You needn't worry. With your help we should get there well ahead of Manera. Even if he can somehow find his way there ahead of us, we can elude men of his sort with relative ease," he replied.

"Aye," Wolf said. "That we can and have more times than I can count. But what if—as an extra precaution—we come in on the southern side of Puerto Rico, rather than sail along the northern coast? We know the area well enough, and surely Manera wouldn't expect us to go all the way around. What if we drop anchor near the trail that leads toward the head water on that side of the island? If we do, we can navigate the river all the way to the beach just west of San Juan. From there we can make our way to and inside the citadel. We can then fetch Margaretha from beneath their very noses and slip back to the ship the same way."

Not as easy as Wolf made it sound. The mountainous terrain they must cross, both coming and going, would be muddy and slippery due to the abundant rainfall the island received. The unpredictable river currents could become an obstacle. The more hostile natives—who contrary to popular belief still lived there in vast numbers—could pose a problem for them as well. They must choose a path that would give *them* the advantage and not Manera. What if they found Margaretha in a weakened condition? That would add additional time as they left the island. Did Lissa know some detail she might've left unsaid that would help them choose the proper path?

"Lissa?"

She didn't even so much as blink in response. Rand tried again.

"Lissa? Are you all right, my lady?"

Though he called her name twice, she clearly hadn't heard him either time. He looked at Wolf, who seemed just as perplexed as he felt. He moved closer, knelt at her side, and took hold of her hand and rubbed it.

"Is she all right?" asked Wolf.

"I don't know. She feels warm. My lady?" He gently caressed the side of her face.

Finally, she took in a deep breath, slowly let it go, and then blinked several times. She dropped her gaze to his and shivered.

"Can I get you anything? Do you need some water?" he asked.

"No, I'm fine, really," she murmured.

"What happened?"

She waved a hand in dismissal. "Nothing. I just—another vision. You needn't worry."

Rand closed his eyes and heaved a sigh. He should have realized. "I'm sorry, did I interrupt you?"

"No." She let go of a small breath and then shrugged. "Well, maybe just a little."

"I'm so sorry," he said. "What did you see this time?"

"A misty forest. One I didn't recognize. The moon and stars filtered through the trees. I could hear the sounds of nocturnal creatures, so the vision definitely takes place at night. Wolf was about twenty paces ahead of us as we—"

"Us?" Rand cut in.

"You, me, and several members of your crew. Wolf halted his steps and gazed to his right for several moments. 'Twas as if he looked for something. He asked Joris to go left of his position and someone else I couldn't quite see to go to the right. Afterward, he beckoned the rest of us forward. Then, as sometimes happens, the vision abruptly changed its course. I saw Armando Manera boarding a ship. He said something to one of the—"

"What kind of ship?"

"I'm sorry, I don't know." She shrugged. "The vessel seemed far smaller than yours, though and the sails were triangular in shape rather than square, if that helps?"

Wolf exchanged a glance with Rand. "Probably a caravel."

Rand scraped a hand across his chin and nodded. "Aye, and that would mean he's looking for speed or he's incredibly lucky to have found such a vessel. Can you tell me what he said or did once he boarded the ship?"

"No, not really. He said something about gold and then I heard you calling me, so—"

"Well, I think we'll use a little wisdom here, and assume he's either on his way to San Juan or will be very soon. Therefore, let's hasten our pace, shall we?"

Chapter Ten

"Hoist anchor and tack sails to the wind," Rand called as the last of the land crew boarded his ship.

He placed a light hand against Lissa's back and turned her toward his cabin. Wolf followed them below deck as Joris took the helm. Once inside the berth, Wolf fetched the navigational charts from the chest. He spread them out across the table while Rand settled Lissa into the nearest chair. Rand then rifled through the stack, extracted the map he sought, and placed it on top of the rest.

"All right, Lissa." Rand pointed toward a small mass of earth surrounded by ocean water on the right side of his map. "This is where we are right now. Puerto Rico is there, and the fortress is right over here on the northeastern tip of the isle. The river Wolf speaks of runs south to north almost all the way across the island and empties into the ocean about ten miles or so from the structure. If we come in through the south side as he suggests—and I think the idea has merit—I'll ask that you position the ship at seventeen degrees latitude, which is down in this general area right along here. Do you think you can do that?"

"Yes, I think so."

"From there, it would take us an additional two days, give or take, before we arrive at our desired destination," he said. "Those two days would give us time to make final adjustments as to our strategy and get a bit of rest before we go ashore. The only other option I can see is to drop anchor somewhere in the more remote areas off the northern coast, such as this area in through here, and bridge the distance on foot. If we choose this option, then perhaps you can move us over here, on a more northern course."

"Yet, how many additional hours or even days would that route take, Rand?" asked Wolf. "If we do that, we must make sure we anchor in a place Manera wouldn't place his spies. And during the delay the Spaniards could bundle Margaretha up, take her aboard a ship, and sail for Brazil."

"That could happen regardless of our path," Rand reminded him.

"Aye, but then we'd have the advantage of an anchored ship on the south side facing Brazil rather than on the north and having to go around."

Rand expelled a heavy breath as he paced the small confines of the room. Finally, he turned about and gazed at her. "The forest you saw in the vision you told us about earlier. Can you describe it for me?"

"Describe it?" she asked. "What do you mean?"

"Would you say mountain or more coastal?"

"More coastal."

"Could you see a river or the ocean from your vantage point?"

"Neither. I just saw an overabundance of trees, overgrown shrubs and wild grass in the shadows. I could feel moisture all around me, but I can't tell you with any degree of certainty from whence that moisture originated. A humid evening, an impending storm, the ocean, a lake—anything could've produced it."

Wolf shook his head. "That doesn't give us much we can go on, Rand."

"Nay, but the closer the water, the more abundant the foliage, right? For now, I'll assume the vision concerns Margaretha and her rescue, since it shifted to Manera. Should that prove accurate, then the river is the course we should follow."

"Then let's get down to business," said Wolf. "We've very little time to plan this out."

"And perfect it," Rand added as he turned toward Lissa. "Now, you must tell me everything you know about the fortress that holds your sister. Even the details you might think insignificant will mean something to us, so don't leave anything out. Now let's start with the outside entrances, shall we?"

"As far as what I've seen in vision, there are two entrances to this fort. The main entrance is in the center of the structure. A set of thick doors is guarded by a heavy, iron portcullis. There is an entrance in the back built in the same way. Of course, a great stone wall protects the entire citadel as I'm sure you know. There are also a large number of cannons along the battlements. You must consider them before we go barging into the place."

"Aye, we know about the cannons. With luck on our side, they'll never have the opportunity to fire them." Rand fetched an inkwell, quill, and parchment for her use. "As best you can, make me a map of the inside. It doesn't have to be perfect. Show me exactly where they keep your sister and all of the entrances leading to it. Then if you can, you must show me the location and strength of the guards within those locations."

Lissa nodded as she picked up the quill. She sketched a rough outline of the inside of the structure. "They have stairways here and one toward the back, right in this area over here. The rounded stairway at the back leads to the tower facing the ocean. A small hallway juts off to the left of these stairs at the halfway point. There are four different chambers along this particular corridor, two on each side. The one that imprisons my sister is the last room on the left."

"Thereby making it far more difficult to free her and at the same time making it far easier to capture *you* should you manage to get all the way inside the place," said Rand. "Clever."

"Does the room they keep her in have an outside window?" asked Wolf.

"No, but there's a gun port off the landing, right here." She marked the area.

"Then perhaps we could use our grappling hooks and enter in through that loophole," Wolf said.

"Is the opening even big enough for a man to get through?" asked Rand.

"A small man perhaps, but not one the size of either one of you. However, if you scale the walls," said Lissa, "the better point of entry would be over here. I don't think they keep guards in this area. At least I haven't seen any in my visions. The gun port just to the left is larger, and it's not that far from Margaretha."

"Can you tell us what's down here at ground level?" asked Rand.

"Just a whole lot of trees, tall wild grass and thorny bushes."

Wolf shot a glance at Rand and grinned. "Excellent way to lose ourselves in the shadows."

"Exactly. However, once we breach the walls, we must limit the number of men. We don't want the guards finding us out before we achieve our objective. In this situation, stealth is the key to our success. We want to get in and out before they even realize we were there."

For the next half hour Rand and Wolf asked her questions. She answered them to the best of her knowledge.

"You must remember I'm giving you only what I've seen in vision, Rand. This may not reflect everything as it truly is. There could be more guards, more hallways, and more rooms than what I've given you here. I can't see around corners, and things may've changed as to the number of men both inside and outside the citadel."

"We'll compensate for that as we finalize each step of our plans, you needn't worry." He gazed at Wolf and cocked his head toward the door. "Let's discuss this with the crew and see what they offer in this intrigue, shall we?"

Lissa stared at the door they closed firmly behind them. The reverberating thud still echoed in her ears. A shiver of apprehension filled both body and soul. He told her not to worry. Yet, how could she not?

Long after Rand and Wolf left the cabin she fretted over their fateful involvement in her current predicament. She should never have accepted their help in the rescue of her sister. Never. Her only excuse for her choice? At the time, her sister's plight had taken precedence over everything else. Would that she could go back in time and change that. She would never forgive herself if something happened to him or to a member of his crew.

Until now, she had taken her visions for granted. She never sought them out nor asked for them to occur. But what she wouldn't give for the power to make one happen right now, one that would give some insight and a little guidance as to the dilemma she now faced. A sigh escaped her lips as she tidied the bed covers and fluffed the pillow for something to do other than pacing.

Then as his pleasant, woody scent wafted up from the pillows, thoughts whisked her to the kiss they almost shared. The way he looked at her just as he tilted her chin upward set her heart on fire. At that moment she would've traded everything she owned, and all the skills she possessed to experience that kiss. No other man she'd ever encountered had affected her quite like Rand Van Locken did. Lissa lowered her head, drew her clasped fingers to her lips, and closed her eyes.

What have I gotten myself into?

A quick rap at the door ended her wayward thoughts. Rand entered and a mischievous gleam filled his eyes as he approached her. His flirty grin left her a bit weak in the knees.

"So, my lovely lady witch, are you ready to take the helm of the *Draeck*?"

She grasped her talisman and nodded. "If you still think it's a good idea."

"Aye, that I do." He glanced down at the pendant and then gazed at her. "But first, tell me how you do it."

"Do *it*?"

"Move the ship an unbelievable distance, I mean."

"Oh. For that I just use the natural power of both the water and varying temperatures of the wind."

"And somehow you can command those elements to obey whatever it is your little heart desires, is that right?"

She laughed. "Well, at least the notion has worked so far, after a fashion, anyway—"

His grin returned as he gave her hand an affectionate squeeze. "So, is it all right if I stay and watch you do your magic, or should I leave?"

"No, you can stay if you wish. You just can't distract me while I'm concentrating on my task," she said.

"Why? Will something terrible happen if I do?" he teased.

"You could find yourself at the bottom of the ocean, *Kapitein* Van Locken, and nowhere near Puerto Rico should you somehow find your way to the surface without drowning."

Rand chuckled as he let go of her hand, and in concession raised both of his to the height of his chest. He stepped back. "All right, I promise I'll behave. For now, anyway."

Not sure as to what he meant by the comment, Lissa didn't reply. Instead, she walked to the table and placed her finger on the map. "Is this where you want to go, then?"

"Aye, anywhere in that vicinity is fine. A few hours in either direction won't make much of a difference."

"All right, let's see if I can get you there."

She took in a deep cleansing breath, cradled her amulet, and placed all of her focus on that specific area of the ocean. To block all outward distractions, she closed her eyes. Her crystal, cold at first, grew ever warmer in her hand. Alongside the warmth its sparkling brilliance would soon intensify. A vast amount of energy rose up and encompassed her entire body. That force filled every particle of her being. In her mind's eye she witnessed the swift crossing of Rand's "Red Dragon." The ship sailed effortlessly over the waves, flying toward their destination like the legendary creature Rand named her for.

****

Fascinated by the spectacle, Rand observed her smallest movements as the minutes passed by. Aye, her physical body stood before him, all but frozen in queenly grace. Yet it appeared her mind traveled elsewhere. For the winsome smile on her lips, he believed she found joy in the journey. What did she see? What did she feel? He suddenly wished he could accompany her on that voyage and witness those things for himself.

Not that he had any true reason to complain. For right now he took pleasure in just being near her, a thing he craved with increasing ferocity. Each day, even each hour that passed, Lissa claimed more of his heart and soul. Soon she would own it all. He didn't have the power to stop it, and even if he possessed that singular power, he didn't know if he'd use it. The memory of her softened gaze and the way her body trembled in his arms just as he would kiss her, gave rise to the hope that she cared as deeply for him as he did her. If only Laurens hadn't chosen that moment to interrupt them, he would know.

If only.

At long last, Lissa stirred. She drew in a deep breath, opened her eyes and gazed at him. "I think we've arrived, *Kapitein*. But perhaps you should verify that with that thing Wolf uses?"

"Care to join me in the discovery?"

The moment she accepted his invitation, he folded his fingers around hers and held her close. He set a slow pace simply for the need to have her to himself a while longer. They climbed the steps and then crossed the length of the ship. The moment they stepped onto the deck, he caught Wolf's attention.

"Wolf, give us a position," he called out.

Wolf retrieved the back staff and positioned it onto his shoulder. All talk ceased. Each member of his crew focused their gazes on Wolf while his first mate made his calculations.

Wolf chuckled as he lowered the instrument and tucked it away. He winked at Lissa before he shifted his attention to Rand. He exaggerated the clearing of his throat. "We're at seventeen degrees, *Kapitein*."

Exuberant shouts and whistles followed the announcement. Everyone converged upon Lissa with questions and comments she couldn't possibly answer all at once. Rand rescued his lady by ordering his men to stop all their foolishness and get back to their posts.

"Shall we watch the setting of the sun from the stern of the ship? Looks like it'll be quite a spectacle."

A smile touched her lips as she glanced over her shoulder and drank in the sight of the scattered clouds in hues of gray and white that promised a spectacular display. "But the sun isn't due to set for at least half an hour, *Kapitein*. Are you sure you can spare the time?"

"For the company of such a beautiful woman? Aye, I can spare it." He dipped his head toward the rear of his vessel. "Come on."

They arrived at their destination without words passing between them. He leaned against the railing. Lissa broke the silence first.

"So, were the members of your crew able to add to your plans then?"

"Aye, that they did. But your question brings up another for which we need an answer."

"What question would that be?"

"You told me earlier Manera captured you while you were deep in concentration. I suppose that meant you were gathering some kind of energy source from around you. Do I have that right?"

"Yes, you do."

"What kind of distraction had you planned for the guards?"

"Fire. A very large one, in fact."

Rand gave her a sideways glance. "You would've burned down the fortification with your sister still in it?"

"No, not the structure itself, just the thicket which is dangerously close to it. The guards would have had to abandon their posts to keep the fire from spreading to the citadel, would they not?"

"Most certainly." He faced the ocean so she wouldn't see his grin. "What did you plan to do next?"

"While they were busy putting out the fire, I would've entered in through the rear of the fortress. Once inside, I would've gone up the back stairs and fetched my sister with no one the wiser. From there I would've boarded the same ship that took me to San Juan and beg the captain's assistance in taking us home."

"Trust me, I know you wouldn't have any problem

whatsoever in dealing with your captain. But tell me, how would you have managed her door and the portcullis, which I must assume are both locked?"

"A locked door doesn't pose much of a problem either."

"I see." He paused for a moment as he imagined such a scene. "So you thought you'd go in all by yourself then?"

She shrugged. "I thought it best at the time. And I didn't have anyone else I could really trust."

The emotion behind her final whispered words sobered him easily enough. He rubbed his thumb over her fingers. "Well, now you do."

She gazed deeply into his eyes. Rand detected a variety of conflicting emotions playing within their beautiful, green depths. If he had his way, he'd respond by taking her into his arms. He'd then give her the kiss that had been stolen from them before. Yet, he would *not* have her believe he sought her affections in exchange for his help.

"Thank you for that, Rand. I find it such a comfort and I—"

He halted the comment with a gentle finger upon her lips. "Though it warms my heart, your gratitude isn't at all necessary. So you needn't thank me or anyone else aboard my vessel. As is always the case, this is something we've *chosen* to do as a crew."

She lowered her lashes and sighed.

"So, back to the diversion," he said. "We'll need one in order to get inside without notice if possible. But rather than fire, I wonder if you can envelop the entire citadel with the same kind of fog in which you shrouded the *Draeck*? I should think one can't locate an adversary one can't see."

"Would you like a bit of wind to mask the sound of your footsteps as well?"

"You can do that?"

"I believe I can."

"Then I'll include that with my order," he teased.

A look of concern entered her eyes. She shifted her gaze toward the horizon and held it there. "Who's going inside the citadel first?"

"I am, Lissa. But don't you worry over me or my crew."

"How can I not worry?"

He let go of her hand and gently caressed the length of her cheek. "Because we've done this kind of thing more often than you might guess. At the risk of sounding boastful, I'll also add we're quite good at it."

A hard swallow followed a slight nod. "Who all is going inside with us?"

"Wolf, Joris, Cornelius, and Laurens are coming inside with *me*. Once we're inside, Joris and Laurens will go down the steps and unlatch the back door. In so doing, my land crew will have easy access to the main hall *should* the need for those additional men arise. To ensure our success, Johannes, Pieter and Conrad will steal onto the battlements and dispatch any men they might find there. They'll then man the cannons, directing them toward the fortress itself. I daresay that'll give us the advantage, should something go amiss."

Her eyes narrowed as she pounced on his first statement. "With *you*? Just *you*?"

"You'll stay hidden in the forest, Lissa. Once you've taken care of your part in this venture, Andries and Antonis will stay behind and watch over you. The rest of us will take over from there. We won't be gone long. In fact, we'll be in and out so fast, you won't even miss us."

She shook her head even before he finished speaking. "No. No I'm not. I'm going inside that fortress *with* you, Rand. There's nothing you can say that'll make me change my mind. What if you need me? What if there's something I can do should something go awry?"

He shrugged as he swung his head to the side. "I can't think of a single situation wherein we would require your help. As I told you before, we plan for all things that *might* go wrong, and find a solution before we encounter it."

"But what if you discover guards down in the main hall? If they're there, I could easily—"

"Not only are we prepared for such an event, we expect it and are prepared. Please don't fight me on this one."

She put her hands to her cheeks, lowered her head, and sighed. "Oh, Rand, don't ask me to do this. I can't just let you go in there without—"

"Shh, it's going to be all right, Lissa. I promise you we'll get inside that building, retrieve your sister, and leave the place without mishap." At once he drew her rigid body into his arms and held her close to his heart. She dropped her head to his chest.

"What if you're wrong? What if something terrible happens to you or a member of your crew and I could've prevented it? I can't live with that. I can't," she whispered.

"Nor could I live with the event, if something

should happen to you. Don't you see? If I allow you to go inside the fortress with me, all my concentration and efforts from that point forward will be on keeping you safe and protected."

"You mustn't worry about me. I can—"

"Nay, despite all of your abilities, I'd still worry over the unexpected. This will divide my attention and make the rescue of your sister far more dangerous than it needs to be for me, my crew, *and* your sister. So, please, don't argue with me. We know what we're doing. You must have a little bit of faith in me, and far more than you've ever had before. I need that more than anything else right now. Please. I am begging you. Trust me and do as I say."

She stepped away from his embrace and locked her gaze upon his. Her eyes blazed with displeasure and a touch of resentment stained her cheeks. She didn't like it, but she would do as he asked. He knew that.

"My trust you already have, *Kapitein* Rand Van Locken. But just so you know, there will come a reckoning more terrible than what you could possibly imagine, should you break it."

The bewitching fire in her eyes anchored her fate.

As the will for restraint dissipated into thin air, he tugged her back into his arms. Without giving her time for reaction or refusal, he joined his lips to hers.

The first kiss, soft, slow, and tender, soon gave way to countless others that expressed far deeper emotions. As she melted into his arms, each subsequent kiss made one thing absolutely certain.

He loved his beautiful lady beyond all recall, just as she—without any doubt whatsoever—loved him. Neither of them said it aloud. Heart spoke to heart. Soul

irreversibly connected with soul.
He could feel it as easily as anything else.

Chapter Eleven

Lissa awoke to the haunting image of the small Taíno child fresh in her mind. She saw her even now. The poor little thing laid still and quiet while the fever ravished her tiny body. Her heart went out to her. Again.

She snuggled a little deeper into her pillow as she considered the consequences of the vision. The scene, whether they were going to or coming from the citadel, made it clear the girl needed her help. Soon. Yet, even now, they battled time. How could she think to waste even one precious moment of it regardless of when the event would occur? But then again, how could she not? Without her help, the little girl would die.

A tap at the door silenced her thoughts.

"Lissa, are you awake?" asked Rand.

Her heart fluttered in response to the mere sound of his voice. "Yes. Just give me a minute to get dressed."

Lissa rose from the bed, slipped into her clothes, and then took a moment to brush the tangles from her hair. She set the brush on the table. "All right, you can come in now."

He flashed a charming grin as he entered. "How's my lovely lady witch this morning?"

She smiled at the affectionate way he addressed her. Lissa found she didn't even mind the term "witch" for the tender way he said it. She dipped her head. "I'm doing very well, thank you."

"That's good. Andries will bring your breakfast in shortly. I thought I'd also let you know, if all goes the way I think it will, sometime within the next couple of hours, we'll drop anchor. We can then head for shore and take your sister out of that wretched citadel."

"Have you eaten yet?" she asked.

He drew his brows together. "Eaten? No, I haven't."

"Then why don't you take a minute away from your duties and have your breakfast with me? I'd love to have your company for a little while this morning."

He eyed her with suspicion. "Are you saying that so you can use your womanly wiles to change my mind about leaving you in the forest with Andries, or—"

"Would it work?"

She took in a breath and held it as he drew her into his arms. The warm flush that filled her belly now spread throughout her body. Then, just as he lowered his lips to hers, he dropped his voice to a husky whisper.

"Nay, my lady. But you can try if you'd like."

The intoxicating kiss swept away all thought or desire for argument. In its place, an insatiable need to make this moment last forever took control. If only she had that kind of power. If only. Her arms traveled upward and around his neck as he held her tighter still.

A rap on the door was an interruption neither of them wanted.

"Aye?" Rand growled out. Yet, all the while, he didn't relinquish his hold.

Andries opened the door with breakfast in hand. His gaze darted back and forth between them. All the while he made a concerted attempt to hide his smile. Despite his best efforts, he failed. Miserably.

"Good morning *Kapitein*, Lissa—"

"Andries, I believe I'll eat in here, this morning. So, if you'd be so kind?" He made the request without releasing her from his gaze.

"Aye, *Kapitein*." Andries set her plate on the table and nodded. "I'll be right back."

The moment the door closed Rand nuzzled the side of her neck and then slowly worked his way up her jaw and toward the corner of her lips. "Now then, where were we?"

Rand didn't give her time to answer before he took full possession of her mouth—nor would she have had the wherewithal to think of one, even if he had.

All too soon, the sound of Andries footsteps alerted them to his return. The man cleared his throat in a most melodramatic manner before he rapped on the door.

Rand heaved out a defeated sigh and released her from his embrace. He cocked his head toward the door and flashed a grin.

"Come in."

Andries bustled about as Rand settled her into a chair and then took the one opposite her. Once the cook had their eggs, smoked bacon and biscuits spread out across the table he swept his hand across the bounty. "Enjoy!"

She picked up her fork and smiled. "This smells really good. Thank you, Andries."

"You're welcome. I'll return later to clear the plates." He gave them a casual salute and then shut the door behind him.

Lissa took a bite of her bacon. "As usual the food

Debbie Peterson

tastes just as good as it smells."

Rand nodded. "Aye. Andries does have a gift when it comes to mixing his exotic seasonings and victuals."

"Has he always served primarily as cook?"

"Not at all. Andries has served in every position you can think of under the rank of captain. He never had the desire to climb any higher than that, though his qualifications wouldn't have hindered him should he have chosen otherwise. But as his body aged, and the normal aches and pains settled in, he opted for the role of cook. I can tell you that not a soul has ever complained over his choice."

"No, I wouldn't think so. Did his wife teach him to cook? I mean, he does have a wife, doesn't he?"

Rand shook his head. "Andries only married once, and it's something he rarely talks about. From what my father told me; he fell deeply in love with a charming woman named Jannetje. He said rarely did one see a love so strong or true than what they shared. They had but two years together. Then during the birth of his first—and as far as I know only child—death took Jannetje along with his infant daughter. He's had no desire to marry anyone else. Not that he's lived the life of a monk since then, I assure you. Therefore, you can remove that sorrowful expression from off your lovely face."

"Well, even so, it's a very sad story. A love like that should last forever."

His penetrating gaze bore into hers. His arm spanned the length of the table as he laced his fingers through hers.

"Aye. A love like that should."

"But then, life offers no one any guarantees, does

it?" she murmured as the awful 'what ifs' assailed her mind.

Rand gently squeezed her hand and then abruptly changed the subject. He filled the rest of their breakfast hour with lighthearted conversation so she wouldn't think about the danger he faced. She knew that. In return, Lissa didn't tell Rand about her visions concerning the child. Not with the heavy weight he already carried. After they ate, she accompanied him onto the deck and waited. In less than one hour's time, Antonis lowered his brass telescope and waved a hand from his seat on top the crow's nest.

"Destination ahoy, *Kapitein*! Awaiting your orders."

"Then drop anchor and ready the boats," Rand boomed. "I want the land crew ready to board in five minutes. All hands staying onboard the ship, mind that you follow my orders to the letter. Does everyone understand that?"

A host of voices answered in the affirmative.

Lissa swallowed past the knot in her throat as Rand entwined his fingers around hers. He gave her a smile that bespoke his confidence.

"Everything will be all right, Lissa. In less than a week we'll have freed your sister from the Spanish and be on our way to Sint-Kruis."

For the swell of tender emotion, she could only nod in return.

Despite Rand's calm assurances, her apprehension increased as the small convoy of boats drew near to the shore. Heavy undergrowth engulfed the island for as far as the eye could see. Somewhere in there, a small group of Taíno natives hid themselves from the eyes of the

Spanish and the world. They would encounter them soon enough. She prayed that didn't occur until after they rescued her sister.

By the time the sun dipped below the horizon, they were well on their way to the river. The higher they climbed the mountain trail that led to the head waters, the more abundant the leafy-green forest with its huge-trunked trees and overhanging vines became. Over the next hour, the gradual sounds of nocturnal bats, frogs, birds and insects accompanied their otherwise, silent journey. As they reached a small clearing, Rand turned to Wolf.

"I think we'll eat in that little glade right there. Afterwards, we'll let the men rest a bit," he whispered. "Once we reach the river, we'll let them sleep for an hour or so before we begin the final leg of our journey."

"Aye, *Kapitein*."

Wolf signaled the men towing the boats behind them. Rand helped her out of the boat and over to a large boulder near the base of a large palm tree. After he cleared away dried shrubbery leaves, broken branches and yellowed fanned fronds, they sat down for what he deemed a well-deserved rest. No one spoke as Andries divvied up the bread and cheese he'd prepared earlier.

While she ate, her gaze took in each of the men she now considered her dearest of friends. Wolf, Joris, Laurens, Johannes and Pieter, Conrad, Cornelius, Andries, Hazael and Antonis, each carried an air of self-assurance. From all appearances, the task ahead didn't concern them in the least. She gazed at Rand and sighed. He responded with a cocky grin and a wink. She could only hope that cockiness wouldn't be his undoing.

After she finished her meal, Lissa headed into the forest in search of a quiet, secluded place while the men discussed the navigation of the river. She didn't wander far.

Lissa grasped her talisman. She closed her eyes and concentrated all her efforts in shrouding the *Draeck* with a dense layer of mist. Her stone grew ever brighter as she envisioned countless droplets of water rising up from the sea. She combined those droplets with a long breath of cool air. The conjured veil encased the ship as well as the entire area surrounding it.

Satisfied with the results, she opened her eyes to the unexpected sight of Rand. He stood in front of her with a scowl on his face and his brows drawn close together. The moment their eyes met, he took hold of her hand and drew her close to his chest.

"Rand—"

"Lissa, what do you think you're doing?" he whispered, as if the very trees had ears.

"I wanted a private place where I could—"

"Lissa, you can't do this. You can't just walk away without letting me know, even if it's for the sake of privacy." He shook his head in frustration. "Coming out here all by yourself is far too dangerous a thing in this region. You have no idea just how dangerous."

"I didn't think I'd cause you so much concern. Truly, I didn't." She lifted her shoulders in silent apology. "I worried over the *Draeck* and thought I'd give her a layer of protection should an enemy ship happen across her path, that's all. In order to accomplish that, I needed a bit of solitude."

He rested his chin on top her head as he sighed. "My men know what to do should they encounter an enemy ship. But even with that, I still could've accompanied you on your errand, isn't that right?"

"Yes, I suppose so. It's just that you were busy with your crew and I didn't think it necessary to bother you for such a small thing. As you can see, I didn't wander far."

His gazed softened as he caressed the length of her face in one gentle stroke. "Bother me? Such a thing is impossible. Didn't you know? Your incredible abilities notwithstanding, nothing on this earth is more important to me than you are right now. Nothing. So, please, for my sake, don't take any unnecessary chances again, all right?"

Then several Taíno men stepped out of the shadows. The dark, golden brown-skinned men wore very little. Their loincloths were accented only by nose rings and necklaces adorned with seashells or brightly colored feathers. The deadly end of their spears threatened as they tightened the circle around Lissa and Rand.

Before she could say anything, Rand's crew burst onto the scene with pistols drawn, cocked, and aimed at the warriors' heads. The large, widened eyes of the Taíno men glanced from one man to another. Some stood defiant. Others seemed confused. Rand's crew would give the natives no quarter. They would respond in kind. She couldn't let that happen—

"No!" She broke away from Rand's arms. "Please, wait! Don't do anything to these men. I must—"

"Lissa," Rand hissed as he snatched her hand and yanked her back to his side.

She whirled around and faced him head on. "Let me speak to them first."

"They won't understand a word you say. The only language they speak beside their own is Spanish," he ground out between clenched teeth.

"I must try. You see, they have a sick little girl in their village. She's dying."

****

Without question, Lissa had a vision of this child she spoke of. The depths of her tear-filled eyes begged for understanding. "If we delay now, Manera might catch up with us, if he hasn't arrived on the island already. We must think of your sister and her welfare. Is she not more important right now than this child?"

She shook her head. "Don't. I must help this little girl, Rand. There is a *reason* I had this vision. Whether for events in the future or something important right now, we must let it play out. We must."

Resigned to the unexpected duty, he shifted his attention to Antonis and cocked his head toward the warriors. "See what you can do."

Lissa drew her brows together. She shot a glance at Antonis before returning her gaze to him. "I don't—"

"Antonis knows enough Spanish to communicate with those who speak the language," he said.

"I understand it far better than I speak it, and it's been awhile since I used it," Antonis clarified. "Nonetheless, tell me what it is you want to be said and I'll do my best to convey your message."

"But what about Johannes, Pieter, or Conrad? Surely they picked up the language while serving aboard the galleon?"

"Nay, their captors refused to let them hear a word of Spanish. They didn't want them overhearing any of their secrets."

Debbie Peterson

She traced her tongue over the top of her lip. "All right, then. Just tell them I've come to heal the little girl. They'll know what I'm talking about."

Rand signaled his men to remain alert as Antonis struggled to get his point across with both words and hand gestures. Each member of his crew responded by selecting a specific target with a subtle hand-signal, should the need for force arise.

The man he assumed led the warriors, glanced at Lissa several times during the discussion. His stoic expression never changed. In response to the uncertainty, Rand wrapped a protective hand around Lissa's waist, while grasping the hilt of his dagger with the other. His gaze never left the man's face.

Finally, Antonis aimed at thumb at the spokesman. "This man is called Abey. We're to follow them to their village. If I understood him correctly, he and his warriors will enter the grounds first and explain our purpose. They'll also see to it that no harm comes to any of us. They believe one of their benevolent gods used his power to bring the beautiful woman to their village to heal the chief's daughter. Lissa's right. The little girl is dying."

"Lower your weapons, men." He gazed steadily at Abey. "All right, tell him to lead the way."

Wolf tossed him a questioning look. He shrugged.

"We'll just have to adapt our plans according to the current situation," Rand whispered. "This isn't anything new. We've made adjustments before."

"Aye," Wolf replied. "Many times, to the benefit of all."

"Other times, not so much," Laurens mumbled.

Rand nodded. "Let's hope it's not the latter. In the

146

meantime, remain on your guard."

During the hour-long trek that took them ever higher through the mountain forest, Lissa collected an assortment of stems, seeds and blossoms from the plant matter on this island. She put it inside the makeshift bag she carried at her waist. The act surprised him somewhat.

"The herbs you carry are not sufficient for your needs?" he asked.

"I could make do with what I have if it becomes necessary. But her body will respond far better and much faster to the herbs found in her environment, and since they're readily available—"

"I see. How long will it take you to heal this child?"

"If all goes well, no more than two days if she's no worse than what I saw," she whispered. She looked up at him then and scrunched her shoulders in apology. "Rand? I'm sorry."

He gently squeezed her hand. "You needn't be. I realize now this is the right thing for us to do. We'll go in, get this task accomplished, and then continue our mission as planned. No harm has been done."

A soft sigh escaped her lips, yet she said nothing more until they entered the Taíno village, secreted away by the verdant mountain trees.

Abey entered the chieftain's hut, a round shelter made of woven straw and palm leaves, supported by wooden poles. It was built far larger than the rounded *bohois* surrounding it, made in like manner. The rest of them waited by the community fire in the center. While they waited, many of the natives emerged from their abodes. They looked them over, but no one spoke.

Minutes later, the warrior emerged. He shifted his gaze toward the gathering of natives on his right and lifted a beckoning hand.

"Yahíma?"

One of the women gazed at each of her companions before she extracted herself from the group and ambled to his side. He put a hand on her shoulder while they whispered in conversation. Many times, her gaze fixed upon Lissa.

Finally, Yahíma gulped and slowly stepped toward them. "The woman has permission to enter the *caneye* of Cacique Alonso. *Only* the woman."

Though surprised she could speak English, Rand didn't dwell on it. Right now, only Lissa possessed his concern, and he would not have her go inside that hut unprotected. He shook his head.

"Not without me, she isn't. If you want her help, then—"

"Rand—"

"Shh, Lissa. This is not open for discussion," he replied. "You'll not go in there alone."

Yahíma whirled toward Abey and relayed his message. Again the warrior entered the hut, this time accompanied by Yahíma. They didn't wait long before the woman appeared in the doorway and invited them both inside with a wave of her hand.

Lissa entered first. He followed a step behind. The little girl Lissa must've seen in vision lay wasting away on the smallest hammock in the far corner of the hut. Surrounded, he assumed, by her family who either sat on the ground on woven mats or on the few wooden chairs that rested inside. They turned hopeful eyes toward his lady. She, in turn, responded with a sweet smile and a nod.

"What's the little girl's name?" asked Lissa.

"Tinima," Yahíma replied. She pointed to the woman holding Tinima's hand. "This is Bacana, her mother."

"That's a very pretty name and suits her well. Tell her my name is Lissa."

The Taíno woman touched her heart and bowed her head.

"I need two pots, one with boiling water and one with cold. I'll also need something I can stir with, as well as a cup, a bowl, and a cloth." Lissa said to Yahíma.

At once Yahíma rushed outside to accomplish her task.

Lissa approached the sleeping child and placed a hand to her flushed cheeks.

Rand rested his hands on Lissa's shoulders and leaned close to her ear. "Is she any worse than what you expected?"

"No, I don't think so, thank goodness."

Minutes later, Yahíma returned with the requested supplies. Lissa opened her bag and dropped selected herbs into the pot of hot water and others into the cold. She stirred and mashed the contents many times over. A sweet scent soon permeated all around them. Lissa poured a bit of the hot brew into the shallow ceramic cup. While it chilled, she bathed the girl's body with the cool mixture of herbs. This would help bring down the fever, she said.

Finally, as the child stirred, Lissa slipped a hand underneath her head. "Come, Tinima," she tenderly whispered. "Drink the tea. It will take away the ache in your tummy and the pain in your body. That's it. That's a good girl. Drink all of it now. See how much better it makes you feel already? Just a little bit more. There you go."

As with Wolf, she repeated the process many times over as the night progressed. Then finally, just before dawn colored the sky with muted shades of orange and red, Tinima drew in a deep breath. For the first time since their arrival, her eyes fluttered open. Her big brown eyes filled with recognition as she gazed at Lissa. A broad smile broke out as she raised her little hand, cupped Lissa's cheek, and said something in her native tongue.

In response, tears filled Bacana's eyes and then coursed down her cheeks.

Rand took in each face filled with silent wonder and gratitude. "What's she saying?"

Yahíma dabbed at a tear and swallowed many times over.

"Our little one tells us that Lissa is her friend. She said that she saw her sailing across the great water in the big boat. Somehow Tinima knew Lissa would come and make her better."

Chapter Twelve

"I must say I'm surprised you're up and about after just four short hours of sleep. Not only are you awake, but here you are, an uncomfortable distance away from the village—alone, I might add—and inspecting the foliage as if you haven't a care in the world."

Rand's voice startled her. Lissa whirled around and all but stumbled into his arms. A guilty flush stained her cheeks as he steadied her.

"Oh, it's just that, well, while everyone slept, I thought I'd gather more of the herbs I used in healing Tinima, that's all."

"I see." Humor filled his eyes even before it became evident in his grin. "Are you expecting another calamity in the very near future? You can tell me if you are—"

"No, no new calamity is on the horizon as yet. But you never know when one might occur, right? As I've said before, I'd rather be prepared for such a happenstance than not have what I need when I need it."

"So, you have." He paused for a moment and then shrugged. "After watching you with Wolf on the island and then with the chief's daughter last night, I think I can understand the need. However, after I awoke this morning and found you missing, I believed I'd find you inside Alonso's *caneye* or with Yahíma in her hut. But

151

as you already know, I didn't find you in either place."

"If it makes you feel any better, I did stop by Alonso's first. Tinima, still deep in peaceful sleep, didn't show any signs of illness. Therefore, I didn't see the harm in collecting a few herbs while she slept."

"That's not the point. The point is, in light of our recent discussion, I don't understand why you didn't wake me up and ask for my company before you left the protection of the village."

"I don't see where it's that much of a mystery. You needed your sleep, and I needed the fresh petals from a plant that only blooms during the early morning hours."

An exasperated sigh accompanied the shake of his head. "Lissa—"

"Come now, Rand. You won't make me apologize for being considerate, will you?" She smiled at him as she placed a hand against his chest. "Besides, you must have had some kind of foresight of your own. After all, I've only been out here a few short minutes, and that's certainly not enough time for anyone to get into any kind of trouble."

"The amount of time doesn't make any difference—"

"Then why argue? Especially on such a beautiful morning. Now, would you scrape some of the bark off that tree right there for me, please? I'd rather not use the sharp side of a rock."

Rand dropped his gaze to the ground. He let loose a defeated sigh before he withdrew his dagger and moseyed toward the small tree with its broad green leaves and gnarly trunk. "You do know this tree is different from the one we found on the island?"

"Yes, but it serves the same purpose." She

approached a small patch of dandelions, rich in vivid yellow hues, stooped down, and collected almost all of them.

"I find it curious you would know that."

She turned away from her task and gazed into his eyes. "Curious? How so?"

"You spent most of your life in the Duchy of Guelders. So how do you know which plants to use for the various ailments in places you've never visited before?"

"For the most part, plants have cousins, so to speak, regardless of how distant the relationship. Although they may look far different, they do have similar distinctions." She rose to her feet and headed toward him with her prize in hand. "For lack of a better explanation, they have common auras or colors that I can either see or feel when I'm around them. Experience has taught me what effect those various auras have on the human body, both good and bad."

"So, this aura you speak of, is seeing or feeling it something you learned from your elders, or were you born with the gift?" he asked as he handed her the prickly shavings.

"A little bit of both, I guess." She stuffed both flowers and shavings into her makeshift bag. "I think all gifts or talents a person is born with, whether that gift is in music, art, leadership, or even in commanding a ship, needs a process of development as the individual matures though, don't you think?"

"Yes, I suppose that's true."

"Then see? The *Witte Wieven* are not that different from anyone else."

He laughed. "I wouldn't go so far as to say that.

You are by far the most unique woman I know. I can't think of a single female who even comes close."

She drew her brows together. "I don't know if I should take that as a compliment, an insult, or a—"

"Definitely a compliment, my lady." He grabbed her hand, gave it a gentle squeeze, and winked. "Definitely a compliment. Now, where would you have us go next?"

She turned toward the sound of rushing water. "There are a few plants that only grow along the banks of the river. I want some of the leaves and stems if you don't mind taking a walk."

"I don't mind at all. Come on."

While they traveled along the twists and turns of the river in collecting her herbs, Rand amused her with stories of his life at sea, before and after he acquired his infamous Red Dragon. Those stories prompted of few of her own that happened in Gelderland. By the number of questions he asked, the accounts of those who crossed over great distances in seeking relief from their maladies intrigued him most.

"How did they even know you existed and that you had this unique set of skills?"

"Word passes from one person who has benefited from our knowledge to another who needs it. Such is the way it's always been."

"I see. Did anyone ever ask for something that set you back on your heels?"

She laughed as a host of such memories flooded her mind. "More often than you might think."

"Like what, for instance?"

"Well, one example happened about a year or so before we left Eefde. A man from Drenthe arrived at our doorstep with what he termed *a vexing problem*. He said his mare refused to mate with a neighbor's prized stallion. Therefore, he wanted us to make him a brew that would make the "stubborn vixen" a little more willing to accept the stallion's advances so that he could get the foal he paid so dearly for."

The story all but doubled him over with laughter, and as minutes passed, the harder he laughed.

"Nay," he said as he finally brought his mirth somewhat under control. "You can't be serious. He actually asked you to concoct some sort of-of love potion for his horse?"

"Yes, he did."

"And did you?"

She dipped her head to the side. "Well, let's just say I did what I could to ease the mare's anxiety and leave it at that."

"You know, sometimes people truly astound me." He turned his gaze skyward. "But love potions don't really exist, do they?"

Her amusement faded. "I'm afraid there are herbs that, brewed in a specific combination, will have that effect. We won't make them the tea, though. People don't understand the consequences of such a request, and even if they did, most of them wouldn't care. Well, at least not while in the frame of mind they're in when they ask for one."

"Consequences?"

"Yes, there are several, but I'll give you one. What if, after time, the person administering the tea finds he or she doesn't love the object of his or her affections after all? That the feeling was naught but a momentary lust or a passing fancy?"

"I suppose that could be awkward for both parties involved."

"Most assuredly. More importantly, we believe and have ever believed that love is something that should never be forced upon one individual by another. Love should come through mutual affection and the tender nurturing of that affection."

"You're an amazing woman, Lissa. Do you know that?"

Lissa lowered her lashes as the heat rose to her cheeks. "Well, it's nice you think so."

Rand caressed the top of her hand. A shiver ran down the length of her spine from his gentle touch. "I must tell you; I'm kind of surprised the men in Eefde let you slip through their hands. Were they too intimidated to, ah, court a woman with your particular skills and background, or did your father bar them from your door under threat of blade, ball, and shot?"

She laughed over the image she conjured of her father guarding the door with sword in one hand and musket in another. Lissa shook her head. "I'm not so sure either situation applies to me. But now that we're on the subject, why didn't you ever marry? I'm certain you've had opportunity aplenty with more than one willing maid," she said as she briefly dropped her gaze to the dress Rand gave her on the island.

In response, he enfolded her into his arms and gazed into her eyes. Just as it always did, the simple way he looked at her fanned the embers that smoldered deep inside her belly. *Would it always be so?*

"You surely know the answer to that question, don't you? I never married because I hadn't yet found you."

Without waiting for a response, he joined his lips with hers. Her hands traveled up the length of his chest and around his neck needing to feel him closer still. That one exquisite kiss drew her deep into an enchantment that she had neither the power nor will to break.

I love you, Rand Van Locken. I love you.

Lissa lost all sense of time and purpose while Rand held her captive in his arms. She gloried in the feel of each kiss they shared. Yet, somewhere in a small corner of her mind, someone called her name. She ignored it for a time, but the persistent voices grew louder and ever more demanding. With more reluctance than she could express, she broke away from the kiss.

"I think someone needs me. Maybe Tinima…"

****

Rand didn't care who wanted her. Their desire couldn't be greater than his right now. For a few more selfish minutes, he retained possession of her rising passion that matched the intensity of his own. In all likelihood, the next opportunity for such a moment would not manifest itself until well after the rescue of her sister.

The sound of approaching footsteps ended their all too brief time alone together. He kissed her one last time, loosed a grudging breath, and released her from his arms.

Tinima bounded through the tall grass, dragging Wolf by the hand. Yahíma trailed a single step behind them. The child, smiling from ear-to-ear, abandoned Wolf and rushed toward Lissa. With a joyful laugh, his lady stooped down and scooped the child into her arms. Though he found it obvious Tinima found delight in

Lissa's company, the child didn't go long without peeking over at Wolf. Each time she did, his first mate winked. The child beamed at him in return.

"Looks like you've made a new friend," Rand said.

"Aye, but I can't explain the why of it." Wolf smiled. "All I can tell you is she entered the *bohio* looking for Lissa. When she spied me, she rushed over, grabbed my hand and wouldn't let go until just now."

Lissa turned her gaze toward him. A mysterious smile turned the corners of her mouth after Wolf's comment, yet Rand couldn't fathom a reason for it. She drew her shoulders together.

"Perhaps she finds you exceptionally handsome, Wolf. Or, maybe she feels some sort of deep connection with you that only she can feel, for now."

"I think what she feels is better." Wolf reddened. "To look at her now, one wouldn't even guess she'd been knocking on death's door."

"Which is a testament to Lissa's gift of healing," Rand replied.

"That it is," Yahíma said. "Just look at her. We didn't think our dear little one would recover, and now she's running about as if sickness hadn't claimed her at all."

"Yes, and in order to keep her that way, she needs a little more tea this morning," said Lissa.

"Are you all finished here then?" asked Rand

Lissa looked down at her bag, once again filled to the top, and patted it. "Yes, I think I have everything I need."

"Then let's go, shall we?"

His lady clung to the arm he offered as they strolled toward the Taíno village. All the while, Tinima chattered on about a variety of things. Yahíma struggled to keep up with the translation. Rand found it amusing.

Upon their return, he and Lissa parted company. She headed for the chief's *caneye* with Tinima and Yahíma in tow, while Antonis beckoned him and Wolf inside Abey's abode. As they stepped inside, he found the small *bohio* already filled with his men and a handful of native warriors talking calmly amongst themselves.

Rand turned toward Antonis and raised a brow. "Is something amiss?"

Antonis waved the question aside. "I don't know. Abey said he had something he must discuss with us. He wouldn't speak of it, though, until you and Wolf returned. The whole thing has tested our patience."

Abey invited them to sit down with no more than a pointed glance at the thick, grass-woven mats. Once they settled comfortably onto the surprisingly soft material, Abey turned his gaze toward Antonis. While the warrior spoke, Antonis listened. At times he interrupted Abey and asked questions. The man answered each of them in turn.

At the end of their discussion, Antonis rubbed his hands together. "All right then. Abey tells of an entrance into the citadel, which leads to an underground channel. He says this tunnel is far safer and far easier to access than is the gun port we thought we'd use. The passageway leads to a drain hole inside the dungeon. A dungeon that is no longer used to house prisoners, they say. In their great desire to repay us for the kindness given the chief's daughter, he and a few of his warrior friends will lead us through the tunnel. They will take us over to a drain hole, into the dungeon and then assist us in retrieving Margaretha from her prison. See there? Lissa's visions had a reason, after all."

"How do they even know about this tunnel when they avoid the area at all costs?" Rand asked.

"He said their grandfathers built the first crude compound during the days they were used as slaves," Antonis replied. "Then years later, after the Spaniards completed the fortress as it now stands, the original dungeon became obsolete. Yet, at the same time, it remains connected to the structure."

"Aye," said Wolf. "But just because their grandfathers dug the thing, doesn't mean the tunnel is still functional. After all these years, the walls might've collapsed or become impassable. They could have sealed the entrance so that—"

"I asked him about that too. He said despite the passing of time, the passageway is still in good repair. They used it less than a year ago when they freed Yahíma from captivity."

"The Spaniards kept Yahíma as a slave?" asked Johannes.

"For more than half her life, he says. Yahíma said she learned our language, among others, from a Spanish priest while in the citadel. The only Spaniard, I might add, that treated her with kindness. Abey tells me they developed a true fondness for one another."

"But that doesn't make sense," said Pieter. "I know the ways of the Spaniards firsthand. They would've pursued Yahíma after her escape. Without question, her trail would've led them to this village. In turn, the soldiers would've massacred the entire Taíno populace, sparing none. After that, they would've burned all their structures to the ground."

"That they would've," agreed Conrad. "They wouldn't in any way treat a perceived enemy with any mercy whatsoever. Here especially, I should think, since they believe they've removed all the native people from the island."

"No, you see the priest was dying, and he knew it. Because of his fondness for Yahíma, he concocted a plan that would free her from her captors. He told the officials she contracted smallpox. They immediately placed her in isolation for fear of getting the disease themselves. After a sufficient number of days, he reported her death and said he would arrange for burial so as not to risk anyone's life but his own. They happily permitted him. However, during that time, he made contact with the Taíno. They came in the dead of night, escorted her through the tunnel, and home, with no one the wiser."

Rand considered the change it would make in their plans if he even allowed the involvement of their new friends.

"What's the distance between the connecting drain and the stairway, which leads to the room that houses Margaretha? Also, what about the guards between the two? Does he know how many men occupy the space?"

Antonis asked Abey the questions. In turn, Abey dropped to his knees and with his finger, drew them a representation of the structure and the path they would take, in the dirt. He didn't know about the guards, for he'd never been all the way inside.

"What about outside?" asked Laurens. "Are there guards near the passage entrance we must contend with before we go inside?"

"Abey said that throughout all the time they watched the citadel, no more than two men patrolled the area," said Antonis. "There were times they saw no one about at all. The Spaniards keep most of their forces in the front of the citadel where ocean marauders are the greatest danger."

Rand turned to Wolf. "We can overtake two men easily enough without anyone else knowing we're there. Even twice that many wouldn't be at all difficult."

"Aye," Wolf replied. "I believe this entrance into the fortress is the better choice. The path is shorter in distance, and we'd surely have the element of surprise if nothing else. I can't imagine they would expect anyone to rise from a drain hole. Before they could recover their wits, we'd have them in our custody."

His men echoed similar sentiments.

"All right then, the tunnel it is. There's just one thing though." He turned his gaze toward the Taino warrior. "Abey, as much as I appreciate the offer, I don't think you or your friends should come with us. Such a thing isn't wise."

As Antonis finished the translation, Abey firmed his jaw. He shook his head in protest as did all his companions.

"They won't have any of it, Rand," Antonis said. "Abey and his friends are resolute about coming inside with us. They are insisting that this is the only way they can repay the debt they believe their tribe owes us."

"Then, they must listen to me before they make up their minds, please."

As Antonis conveyed his message, Abey folded his massive arms against his chest.

"The Spaniards believe they have either killed all

your people or removed those that survived to their various colonies," Rand said. "This is a good thing. Since they no longer believe your people are here on this island, they're not looking for or hunting your people down. We must keep it this way for the sake of your women and children. There are not enough warriors here in the village that can stand against the army the Spaniards have gathered here. I'm sure you see the wisdom in this."

Abey said nothing as Antonis told the Taino men what Rand said. The warrior's expression remained stoic. Nonetheless, Rand pressed on.

"We do ask that you guide us to the passageway. This act, and the risk you'll take in this part of the venture is more than enough compensation for the care given Tinima."

The Taíno warriors bade them wait while they stepped outside and discussed his arguments amongst themselves. The wait didn't take long. Upon their return, Abey informed Antonis of their decision.

Antonis placed a hand on Abey's shoulder. "They'll do as you've asked, Rand, on one condition. Abey and his men will escort us just shy of the tunnel entrance. Then they'll fall back. However, they insist on staying in the area. They'll wait long enough to ensure our safe entry in and out of the passageway just in case they can be of further service. Once they see you return and know all is well, they'll head back to the village."

Rand offered Abey his hand. The warrior instantly grasped it.

"You have our deepest gratitude. Now, come, my friend, let's get this thing planned out. We must do it without overlooking the slightest detail."

Chapter Thirteen

The brilliance of the morning sun faded away. The delicate perfume carried by the breeze disappeared into the deepest part of her mind as well. Lissa could no longer hear the birds in the boughs high above her. For now, other voices overtook her thoughts as the gathering mist stole her attention. Yet, she couldn't make sense of the words that were spoken in such hushed tones. Lissa mentally moved ever nearer the sound until she could hear the conversation.

Manera!

She could finally see him now too. He had his head down and was deep in discussion with the man at his side. They strolled down a darkened hallway. The stone walls told her the conversation took place inside the citadel. She now recognized his companion as the more mysterious accomplice she had seen in an earlier vision.

Armando halted, turned and faced his cohort as he huffed out a scathing breath. "Are you certain you've seen nothing that would indicate her return? She must come back here. There's no doubt about that. She wouldn't leave her sister languishing inside prison walls. Such is not her way. You've already seen that much for yourself."

Enshrouded in a dark-gray cloak, the man with toad-like features shrugged away the notion. "Be that as it may, we've not seen a single ship anywhere near the harbor since you set sail with your prisoner in tow. The fact that you let her slip through your grasp is most unfortunate, but not unexpected, Armando."

"What do you mean? We took every precaution. If not for the Dutch captain of the Rood Draeck *we would've—"*

"Would she not have found a way regardless? She managed to slip onboard the ship that transported her here without notice by the captain or her crew. An amazing feat all by itself, wouldn't you agree? Then, when questioned, the gullible fools denied giving her or any other woman passage. They insisted that beside the crew, they saw naught but a ghostly apparition shrouded in mist during the voyage, and only then on a rare occasion or two. The manifestation scared them out of their wits or would have if they had any. Why, if not for the indiscretion of your favored guard, and his illicit midnight tryst in the forest, we wouldn't even have known the girl stepped foot on this island. Therefore, it should come as no surprise to either of us that she placed some kind of evil spell upon the Dutch capitán and all those aboard his ship."

"But the symbols alongside the blessed herbage should have prevented the use of her powers. You assured me of this," Armando whined.

"Once inside the berth, indeed they did. You needn't doubt the truth of that. But you're forgetting that she could've cast her spell well before we brought her aboard the galleon. Perhaps she selected the ship intending it as her means of escape once she rescued her sister." He waved an impatient hand. "Never mind all of that right now. What's done is done. However, in light of our current circumstances, I think we should

present the sister in place of Lissabeth as our best course of action. Though she lacks the superior skill of her sister, Margaretha could still be useful to the king if Lissabeth somehow eludes our grasp. We'll simply tell the officers and guards we've been commanded to escort Margaretha to Spain instead of Brazil. That she's to face the Inquisition there, and we need to send her as soon as possible."

"Will they believe such a lie?" Manera asked.

"Don't be absurd. They wouldn't dare doubt my word."

"What if Lissabeth returns beforehand?" he asked.

"Should we reclaim the witch, we'll present them both to the king."

Manera gasped. "But you said it was dangerous to place the two of them together, that they could then combine their power and work their wicked spells against us."

"We'll never let them see each other."

"You forget that Lissabeth has frequent visions. She'll know—"

"Not once we shield ourselves from their evil by a power far greater than their unholy demons. Furthermore, we'll make each one believe the other's life is at stake should they not comply with our wishes."

"I don't know. What if Capoen finds out? We'll surely face the wrath of the Dutch military forces if he learns we're responsible for taking both—"

"Silence! For Benavides's sake, and both our sakes, it's a risk we must take. Now do as I say or suffer the consequences."

Manera gulped and dipped his head. "I'll arrange passage on one of our ships straight away."

"Don't forget to take all necessary precautions before you take her onboard. We underestimated Lissabeth. Let's not make the same mistake with her sister. Remember, you, and you alone, will be held accountable should we lose this one."

"I give you my solemn oath, Margaretha will be presented to the king. I'll see to it. In fact, I'll—"

Manera's chilling vow echoed inside her mind as the swirling haze closed in around the vision and then dissipated. When she opened her eyes, Lissa gazed at the child who napped in her arms. All traces of the illness that had threatened Tinima's life had fled and wouldn't return. Indeed, the little one spent most of the afternoon yesterday with her playmates as they sang and danced in celebration of her recovery. When the games ended, her little friend once again sought her out.

Throughout the remainder of the day, Tinima shadowed every step she took. Not that she minded. She found her a delightful companion with a thirst for knowledge. A thing that would serve her—and her great posterity—well into the future. Especially one in particular.

But now, a need for them to stay in the village no longer existed and they were running out of precious time. With a sense of urgency, Lissa stood up and transferred the child to Yahíma's arms. Although curiosity filled the woman's eyes, she didn't ask any questions.

She gave her an apologetic smile. "I'm sorry, Yahíma, but we must go now. We've tarried far too long in your village. Do you know where Rand is?"

Yahíma pointed to the chief's hut. "He's inside the *caneye* of *Cacique* Alonso with some of his men."

Rand stepped out of the hut with Wolf, Joris, Johannes, and Laurens a single step behind him. As their eyes met he lifted a brow and frowned.

"What is it Lissa? What's wrong?"

"We must leave right now. I saw—"

"Manera?"

She swallowed past the dryness in her throat and nodded. "Yes."

"He's here?"

"I'm not sure. He could very well be. I can but hope he hasn't yet arrived. All I can tell you for certain is that once he gets here, he and his accomplice will put Margaretha on a ship bound for Spain. They'll present her to the king in my stead. So we must leave the village. Today. Now."

"Actually, we've made plans to do just that. I was just coming to get you, so you could prepare. I also thought I'd tell you that Abey and a few of his friends will come with us."

She glanced at the warriors who had joined the members of Rand's crew. "They are? Why?"

"Because yesterday Abey told us about a secret way into the citadel. In gratitude for the service you've rendered the chief's family, they'll go with us. They'll show us the location of the tunnel's entrance. The point of entry is below ground level and is far easier for us to breach than the gun port. Besides the company of the warriors, he'll provide us with dugout canoes for the journey. They move much faster through the water than do our boats. We'll save a lot of time if we use them."

"Is the passage he speaks of guarded?"

He shrugged away her concern. "At times, but never by more than two and only then because they guard the tower, not the tunnel. Abey isn't sure they even know the tunnel is there. But whether they do or not, once you create that shield of wind and fog, we can capture them easily enough should we find them there."

She bit down on her lip. "How soon can we leave?"

"I don't think it will take our friends more than an hour and perhaps just half that to gather the supplies they need."

"Good, we must hurry. I fear our time is running out."

The same warriors that had escorted them to the village now led them through the deepest parts of the forest, heading toward the river that would take them to the fortress. All the while her heart increased its pace and so did her worry Did the disquiet mean Manera had made port rather than sailed toward it? Throughout the endless trek, Rand reassured her many times over with nothing more than a wink or the gentle pressure of his hand on her waist. Yet the gestures didn't ease her anxiety.

At long last, the sounds of the river cut through the stillness of the woodland with its many yews, palm and kapok trees. Abey held up a hand. Everyone stopped in their tracks and waited for further orders. Abey leaned toward Antonis and whispered something she couldn't hear. In turn, Antonis gazed at each member of Rand's crew.

"We'll stop here and take a little rest before we navigate the river," he said. "A word of caution. Speak only in hushed tones if you find conversation necessary and be on your guard. On rare occasions, the Taíno have spotted the Spaniards very near this area. However, this far away from their base, and this late in the day, they don't expect we'll encounter anyone."

The moment they settled in an area hidden by shadows, Lissa glanced at each of the men while Andries rummaged through his food sacks. Conrad and Cornelius helped him distribute the evening meal which consisted of no more than bread and cheese.

"How long do you think it will it take us to get to the fortress from here, Rand?" she murmured.

"If all goes well, Abey believes we'll arrive shortly after nightfall," he said.

"If you think about it, the timing coincides with the vision you told us about, Lissa," Joris whispered. "We'll take that as a good omen."

Johannes nodded. "Aye. We'll be in and out of the citadel in no time at all."

"So you all keep telling me," she said.

Rand shook his head. "You're worrying needlessly, Lissa and don't tell me you're not, because I can see it in your eyes. Everything will go just as we've planned. Trust me."

"You don't know that. If Manera arrives before we do, everything will change, and all your plans will be for naught."

"Not true." A gleam leapt into Wolf's eyes. "We're prepared for every possible situation, most especially Manera's return."

"Look," said Rand. "Even *if* Manera is on the island, he still must prepare the ship. They'll need fresh water and supplies a plenty for such a long voyage. Don't forget; just as he did for you, he'll feel he must fashion one of those bizarre berths for Margaretha. It will take additional time as they carve the symbols, gather whatever that foul foliage is that they believe will obstruct her powers, and hang them around the door."

"But what if it's already done? What if we're too late?" she whispered.

Rand placed a curved finger underneath her chin, tipped her face upward, and gazed into her eyes. "We're not too late. Don't let such a thought trouble you. You forget; you gave us far more time than what fate allotted Manera. You've also given us details about the plans we wouldn't have had otherwise. That gives us the definite advantage in this situation."

"As I've told you before, those plans can change in a heartbeat," she said.

"I don't believe that's the case with Manera. The man isn't that intelligent. I mean, what kind of idiot would abduct a woman he believes is a genuine witch of all the foolish things? Even more foolish? He'll try again."

Yet, despite their light-hearted banter and calm assurances of Rand's crew, her apprehension grew. Once Abey decided they had rested enough, they headed for the riverbank.

Upon arrival, she and Rand, accompanied by Wolf, Joris, Laurens, and Johannes, boarded the first canoe piloted by Abey. Pieter, Cornelius, Conrad, Andries and Antonis boarded the second. The rest of Rand's crew traveled behind in the third canoe. In the tedious hours that followed, the Taíno warriors maneuvered through the twists and turns of the river with skillful ease. The shadows caused by the setting sun didn't hinder their ability. Then just as she wondered if they'd ever get there, Abey turned his canoe toward the bank of the river. She gazed at Rand and lifted a brow.

"Abey told us that once we leave the river, the fortress will be no more than twenty minutes away. We'll travel the rest of the way on foot," he whispered in response to her unspoken question.

The beat of her heart accelerated as they disembarked. The men retrieved the arsenal of weapons from out of the boats and passed them out with a nonchalance that unnerved her even further. Each man outfitted himself with a sword, a number of daggers and loaded pistols. Once armed, they grabbed their supplies and followed the warriors into the forest. Abey had his men fan out as they scouted the area ahead. After giving them a significant head start, he beckoned them forward and disappeared into the shadows created by plant life and trees.

Then, just as she had witnessed in her vision on the island, Wolf advanced through the woodland first. Joris and Johannes flanked him. She and Rand followed next while the rest of the land crew lagged behind. The sounds of nocturnal birds calling out to each other eclipsed the sound of their footsteps as they drew ever nearer the citadel. With each passing step, the danger she sensed increased the pace of her heart. If not Manera, then surely the feeling arose from the close proximity of his spies. Did the Spaniards see them even now?

She glanced over her shoulder. Rand's crew still followed. Pieter and Conrad gave her a reassuring nod. After returning the gesture, she gulped and faced forward. At about twenty paces ahead, Wolf halted his steps. For several moments his gaze swept over their environment in search of the slightest threat to their mission. He then sent Joris left of his position and

Johannes to his right. Once in place, he beckoned the rest of them forward. Rand wrapped a hand around her waist, drew her close to his side and nestled his jaw against her cheek.

"We're almost there," he murmured. "Are you ready?"

She grasped her pendant and held it close to her breast. "Yes, I am. Are you?"

He stopped and turned her toward him. "We've gone over the maps you and Abey have given us a thousand times. We can walk the perimeter and interior of the entire citadel in our sleep without any trouble whatsoever. Don't worry, Lissa. Just give us the cover we need, and we'll do the rest."

"All right." She hesitated for a moment and then placed her hands on top of his arms. "Rand? Please be extra careful."

A slight grin turned a single corner of his mouth. "Always."

He dropped a sweet kiss on top of her lips before they resumed their journey. It didn't take them long. Just up ahead, Abey and his warriors awaited them near the edge of the forest. When the last of the land crew stepped into the circle, Abey gazed at her and nodded.

Lissa looked up at the evening sky; all the while a thousand different 'what if's' tortured her mind. Yet, a voice inside reminded her that Rand had asked for her trust and argued that the captain of the *Rood Draeck* had earned it many times over. His skill, his intelligence, and his ability proved him quite capable of carrying out this quest.

With pendant in hand, she closed her eyes. Her mind's eye gazed out over the vastness of the ocean just off the northern coast of the island. She called up a thick, dark cloud that rose out of the water. Her crystal grew ever warmer in her hand as she concentrated on the gradual increase of her creation's height, length, breadth, and density. The elements surrounding her came together just as she envisioned.

Once the thick fog shrouded the entire fortress and every living thing within a quarter mile or so of the grounds, Lissa blew a breath of air against it. Then created a swirling vortex that battered the trees and bushes. She included an image of Rand and his crew as they went inside the citadel. The wind and fog would cover them until they returned and were well past the outer walls. Afterward, the mist would slowly evaporate. The winds would calm, and all would return to its normal state.

Lissa opened her eyes and brushed the wind-blown hair away from her face. The Taíno warriors and every member of Rand's crew met her gaze with something akin to awe. The attention made her a bit uncomfortable. A ragged breath escaped her lips.

"My task is done. I guess the rest is up to you."

Rand kissed the top of her head. "We'll be back before you know it."

As he stepped toward the mist, he stopped. He turned back, looked first at her and then at both Andries and Antonis in turn. "I'm counting on you two to keep her safe. Understood?"

"Don't you worry, *Kapitein*; we'll take good care of her," Andries replied.

"Aye, that we will," echoed Antonis. "You can count on it."

"I am."

The moment Rand disappeared into the haze alongside his men, Lissa regretted the agreement she'd made with him. She shouldn't have let him talk her out of going. All of the 'what ifs' returned and bombarded her mind as the minutes passed. The unexpected flutter of wings, each croak made by frogs, the chirp of birds and whatever insects could be found in this forest unnerved her. What if Spanish guards patrolled this area? What if they captured Rand and his men? Would they shoot them on the spot or imprison and torture them simply for the sport of it? Lissa dipped her head and buried her face in her hands. She should never have let them come to this place.

"Come now Lissa, we'll have none of that," Antonis murmured. "They'll be fine, I assure you."

As she dropped her hands, she swallowed past the knot in her throat and met his gaze. She couldn't speak, so she simply nodded.

Andries approached her then. He picked up both her hands and gave them a gentle press. "Don't worry so much, Lissa. Rand has faced far more dangerous situations than this and lived to tell the tale."

Aye," said Antonis, "and to my knowledge, Rand has never failed in achieving whatever goal he sets himself. I've witnessed that more times than you can count."

Lissa took in a deep breath as she gazed into the deepening fog. "Well then, let's hope this particular task isn't his undoing."

Chapter Fourteen

Abey cut a jagged path through the vast tangle of tall bunch-grass as he led Rand and his men toward the hidden tunnel. Several minutes passed before they stepped onto higher ground and a much better view of their surroundings. The breeze Lissa conjured carried the taste of salty brine, even if he couldn't see the ocean from whence it came. Still, the taste as well as the scent told him they were close to their destination and a parting of the ways with their Taíno friends. Thus far, all had gone just as they had planned.

After they crossed another quarter mile or so, Abey halted near a mound of dirt embedded by boulders and hunkered down behind them. The Taíno warrior formed a V with his fingers and bade him look between them. He peered through the drifting haze, seeking the targeted position. Despite the shrouded light of heavenly orbs, he spied the small rocky passage Abey had described in detail.

The tunnel appeared as no more than a shadow beneath the northeast tower of the citadel. An overgrowth of thick, leafy fronds cascaded down the embankment and over the wall. The excessive vegetation spoke of its lack of use by the Spaniards, if they'd ever used the passageway at all. He scanned the area in search of guards and didn't find a single one. But that didn't mean those conditions couldn't change in a single heartbeat. The quicker they completed this task, the better off for everyone concerned, especially Lissa. He didn't how long Andries and Antoinis could keep her feet planted on the ground.

He and Abey rose to their feet. Rand clasped the warrior's forearm and nodded with gratitude and respect. Abey returned it in kind. Then he and his companions disappeared into the mist.

After their retreat, Rand signaled his men forward. Johannes, Pieter, and Conrad headed for the battlements, to scale the walls with grappling hooks, then take command of the cannons. Wolf, Joris, Laurens, and Cornelius followed him toward the cave entrance, while the land crew fanned out and flanked them. They would guard the perimeter unless called upon to help them inside the citadel.

Rand made use of the shadows as he led his men toward the entrance of the passage. He dropped to his knees and inched his way through the small cavity. Once inside, Joris lit the torch he carried and then held it aloft. The rocky corridor spanned no more than two feet in width and seven feet in height along the twists and turns of the dank channel. A tangle of roots protruded from the walls. By necessity, they would move single file. Yet, the lack of breadth would be most advantageous on the return journey should the Spaniards discover them and be so foolish as to pursue.

He grabbed the torch and cocked his head toward the darkest recesses of the tunnel. "Let's get this done."

"Aye, I'm all for that," Wolf breathed out as he fell into step behind him. "This place stinks to high heaven."

"We've endured far worse," Joris murmured.

Cornelius nodded. "So we have."

"Just because we've endured worse doesn't mean we should linger any longer than we must," said Laurens.

They made their way to the first junction and turned right. The foul air grew ever more putrid as they followed the path to its end. Rand passed the torch off to Wolf and then grabbed the corroded bars overhead. He shook them loose, tossed the grate off to the side, and pulled himself up through the hole. With a hand on the hilt of his dagger, he crouched down and looked about the darkened dungeon. Rusted bars of the individual cells were all but torn from their hinges. Stones that made up the walls had tumbled to the ground long ago. Just as Abey said, no one guarded the area. Then again, he saw nothing of worth they must guard.

"All clear," he whispered as he headed for the crumbling stairs.

He climbed up the steps to the dilapidated doors at the top. By the time he took firm hold of the latch, his men had gathered behind him. Rand nodded the all-clear and opened the door just wide enough so they could pass through. From all appearances, the deserted hallway led to the gatehouse. The place hadn't seen a human inhabitant for quite some time.

"Stay alert," he said.

They prowled through the corridor on silent footsteps. Boisterous conversation at the end of the hall bade them stop just outside the entrance. Rand listened then held up six fingers. Wolf nodded then he and Cornelius moved to his right. Joris and Laurens took positions at his left.

With a firm grip on his dagger, Rand rushed through the door.

His boot slammed into the face of the startled guard closest to him. The Spaniard flew backward and hit the man behind him. The four still on their feet, and the dazed men on the ground, grabbed for their pistols. Daggers whizzed through the air in the same instant the Spaniards swung their weapons aloft.

The scurvy men didn't have time to set off a single shot. After they retrieved their weapons, Rand and his men headed for the tower stairs and crept up them. At the second floor landing they turned left and followed the deserted hallway to the last room on the left-hand side. The door stood ajar. No one occupied what he could see of the chamber. Naught but a few rats skittered across the floor.

"She's not here," Joris muttered through clenched teeth. "We're too late."

"Nay, it isn't too late," Wolf replied. "Look at the food in the bowl. The gruel is still fresh enough. She can't have been gone long. No more than an hour, I'd say, if even that."

Rand whirled about. "Let's find her. Perhaps she's still inside the citadel."

Rand brushed past his men and strode down the hallway. He ignored the tower stairs in favor of the staircase that led toward the great hall below. Just short of the landing, a door opened. A Spanish officer stepped out into the corridor. Rand grabbed the man by the scruff of his neck and slammed him against the wall. He jabbed a pistol underneath his chin. The Spaniard sucked in a deep breath. Rand cocked the hammer and shook his head.

"I wouldn't yell if I were you. As you can see, you will be the first to die," he hissed.

With eyes bulging from their sockets, the man gulped and nodded.

"That's better. Now that I know there isn't any misunderstanding between us, where is Margaretha Capoen?"

"I… I don't know," he stammered.

Rand thrust the barrel deeper into his chin. "Wrong answer. Care to try again?"

"*Por favor, señor*… she is… uh…" He licked at his lips as his gaze darted back and forth along the length of the hallway.

"I've no qualms in ending your miserable life here and now. I can and will find her without you."

"They are… they are taking her to the ship," the Spaniard mumbled.

"Who? Who's taking her to the ship?"

"Armando Manera and *Padre* Lorenco de la Casas."

"*Padre* Lorenco de la Casas?" Rand sneered at the officer. "Now why doesn't that surprise me. Another ambitious maggot who'd like nothing more than to elevate his status in the eyes of the Church, I presume?"

The man said nothing.

Rand huffed out a breath. "When did they leave the citadel?"

"Not long…" He shrugged. "I don't… perhaps fifteen *minutos*."

Rand dragged him over to the nearest gun portal and pinned him against the wall. He gazed toward the ocean as he held out a hand.

"Joris, fetch me the telescope."

With instrument in hand, he peered out through the opening. Through the drifting mist, he spied the silhouettes of three ships moored near the harbor—two galleons—and in all likelihood, the very caravel Lissa saw in the vision that transported Manera to the island. The Spaniards would need far more than fifteen minutes to span the distance between the shore and the vessels.

Added to his relief, he didn't see a single boat taking them there. That meant Manera and Margaretha were still somewhere on the island. He had but a single option open right now, and despite the likely consequences of that action, it was one he must take.

"Joris, run up to the battlements and tell Johannes to blow those ships out of the water. In the meantime, we'll make sure our friend here stays out of trouble. Meet us outside once you give the order. We'll go after Manera."

The Spanish officer lifted his chin and boldly met his gaze. "You're wasting your time. The witch is under heavy guard. You'll never get close enough to—"

Rand ended the taunt with a heavy blow to the back of the man's head. Wolf and Cornelius helped him drag the man's unconscious body to the gatehouse.

Wolf retrieved his knife from his belt and cut off a piece of rope from a coil tacked to the wall. Cornelius bound his hands. They then secured him to the chains that hung from the heavy wooden posts.

Rand cocked his head toward the door. "Let's go."

Just as they stepped outside the fortress, the first sounds of cannon fire roared from the battlements.

Six more shot off in rapid succession as the crew gathered. With a wave of his hand, Rand led his men toward the ocean.

"You don't suppose Lissa will come charging through the foliage in response to the cannon fire, do you?" asked Wolf.

Rand shook his head over the troubling thought. "I hope not. Right now we must trust that Andries and Antonis can somehow hold her fast until our return."

Abey and his warriors burst through the forest with Antonis at their side. As Rand opened his mouth, Antonis lifted a hand and halted his words.

"Before you even say it, Rand, please know that I couldn't talk them out of coming back, no matter how hard I tried. All things considered, I thought I'd better come along and help with translation."

"I see," he said.

Antonis shifted his gaze toward the smoke drifting skyward. "So, what's going on?"

Rand ignored the question for the moment. "Lissa?"

Antonis sucked in a breath through his teeth, squeezed his eyes shut and shuddered. "As you can imagine, she didn't take the sound of cannon fire well, either. I thought perhaps Andries and I would have to tie her to a tree. But then the more I thought on that idea, the more foolish it seemed. I just didn't think it wise to get on her bad side, because, well, you know."

"Excellent decision on your part," said Rand.

"Aye. So instead of risking her wrath, I promised I'd return and give her a report if she remained hidden a while longer. If after my return she still felt she should follow you, then I told her we'd all go. With a whole lot of reluctance, she agreed. At least for now."

"Then tell her this. By the time we entered the

fortress, we found the Spaniards had already taken Margaretha out of her chamber. The officer we captured said Manera had just left with his prisoner, on their way to the ships moored in the harbor. We'll catch up with them soon enough. We shouldn't be long and don't need her help."

"Ah."

Antonis gazed at Abey and told him what Rand had said. A short conversation between the two of them followed.

"Abey believes you'll need an experienced tracker who can follow the Spaniards through the jungle. He said it's obvious they won't return to the citadel under threat of attack. Abey will take on this duty, either with your consent or without it, I'm afraid."

Rand shrugged. "All right, we'll take Abey, but only Abey. Tell our friends we still must protect their people and their village. Should the Spaniards catch sight of Abey, we can tell them he's either crew or a slave. I would also appreciate it if those remaining behind, would watch over Lissa. That is the most difficult part of this mission right now, I'd say."

Antonis made quick work of the translation. "We have an agreement."

"Good." Rand put a hand on Cornelius's shoulder. "Since we'll need Antonis, I'll ask you to watch over Lissa in his stead. And by all the saints, do everything in your power to keep her right where she is."

The emphatic order produced a grin. "Aye, *Kapitein*. If all goes well, I'll see you back at the forest. If you arrive and we're not there, look around for a toad that shadows your footsteps, because it will probably be me."

Chapter Fifteen

The shadows grew as Rand and his men trailed Abey into the deepest parts of the forest. Despite the darkness, the warrior seemed sure of his path. Every so often the warrior would stop, inspect the ground or branches and adjust his course. At length, he slowed his steps and whispered to Antonis.

"Abey tells me we're almost upon them," Antoinis said in hushed tones. "He's counted at least fifteen different sets of footsteps along the way. They've not fanned out but have remained tight together all throughout their journey. He tells me such is their way even when they stop and take a rest. One set of those prints, in all likelihood, is Margaretha's, for the size and weight that makes the depression. If this is true, she has men in front of her as well as behind her at all times, so she's well-guarded."

"If we assign two sets of those footprints to de la Casas and Manera, that means we have twelve guards we must take down when we find them. Keep that in mind when we overtake their company. Find Margaretha before we overpower them. We may have scant seconds to take advantage of their surprise. Whoever is closest to Margaretha, get her out first. Understood?"

"Aye," whispered Antonis. "From here on out, we must carry on with far more caution. Abey believes

that, with the lateness of the hour, and the slower pace, they may be looking for a place to camp for the night."

"All right, men," said Rand. "Be on your guard and have your weapons ready. Should the opportunity arise, we'll surround them with weapons drawn. That will make our position all the stronger."

Abey beckoned them onward.

Finally, Rand put a hand on Abey's shoulder. He moved ahead of the Taíno warrior and focused on the church hidden in the shadow of trees. The broken windows and splintered wood doors said the place was deserted, even though the tracks of the Spaniards ended at the door.

With a hand signal, he ordered the land crew to surround the building. Then, with weapons drawn, he and the rest of his men stealthily approached the broken, wooden door. For a moment he stood just outside the barrier and listened. He heard nothing that indicated Manera, or any member of his company, hid inside. With slow deliberation, he opened the door and stepped over the threshold. Scant light from the moon and stars seeped through the dusty, narrow windows. Rand entered the nave first and gazed about the empty room. As he stopped beside the dilapidated confessional booth, a shadow sprang from the doorway. Moonlight bounced off a large knife in the assailant's hand a second before the man plunged the knife deep into Rand's chest.

He sucked in a breath as he wrapped his hand around the hilt. Burning pain shot through his chest and then radiated outward. Icy cold followed. He yanked the dagger out as he slumped forward. The voices of his men shouted out as a rush of footsteps surrounded him. He couldn't breathe. The sounds faded as did the light—

****

Lissa gasped She bounded to her feet and rushed forward. Andries wrapped strong arms around her waist, halting her flight. He turned her around.

"What is it Lissa? What's wrong?"

Before she could tell him what she had seen, Cornelius rushed headlong through the tangle of trees with the Taíno warriors at his side. He took in several deep breaths as he strode toward her.

"You needn't look so terrified Lissa, it's just us and all is well," he said.

She shook her head and raised a hand toward the thicket. "No. No, Cornelius, it isn't. Rand's—"

He put gentle fingers on her lips. "But it is, Rand is the one responsible for the cannon fire, not the Spaniards. Manera had left just minutes earlier, mind you, with Margaretha in tow. The Spanish officer we came across told us they were taking her to a ship moored in the harbor. Rand stopped them. Antonis and the warriors caught up with us. Abey said he could follow their tracks. They're well on their way now. I don't think it'll take them long to catch up and fetch your sister. So you see? All is well."

Lissa shook her head as she struggled for release. "No, Cornelius, all is not well. I must catch up with them *before* they arrive at that church. I must stop them from going inside. If I don't, Rand will die!"

Cornelius gaped at her. Andries loosened his hold. Yet, as she stepped away the cook grabbed her hand and drew her back to his side.

"Church? What church? What're you talking

about?" Cornelius asked.

"There's a church—oh, I don't have time for explanations, Cornelius. I've got to go. Now!"

She yanked herself free of Andries' grasp and hurried toward the fortress. Did the Angel of Death think he had a claim on Rand for one reason or another? Would he try to take him away from her again and again? No, she wouldn't have it! She stopped him once, she would do so again and a thousand more times if necessary. No power was strong enough to take him away from her. She loved him too much—

"Wait a minute, Lissa," said Andries. He blocked her path. "You can't just take off by yourself! Do you even know where you're going?"

She looked off into the distance. "Abey led them west of the citadel, through the trees. They stayed away from the beach for whatever reason, but I could still hear the roar of the waves. He's leading them to a church that's not far from the shore. Once they arrive, Rand will walk inside and then he'll—"

"Hold, Lissa. Please."

Cornelius gripped the Taíno warrior closest to him and pointed west. Then he dropped to his knees, grabbed a sharp rock, and drew a crude depiction of the citadel with a church to the left of it.

The eyes of the warrior called Macuya lit up in recognition. He turned toward the southwestern portion of the island and nodded.

"*Sí, iglesia.*"

With a frantic wave of his hand, Cornelius begged the man to show them the way. As if sensing the urgency, the Taíno took the lead. At once they moved swiftly through the trees. Lissa didn't have any trouble keeping up with the grueling pace he set. Not when the vision of Rand's death remained fixed in her mind. When Macuya insisted they stop for a short rest, she protested despite her fatigue.

"No. We must keep going, Cornelius. I must get there before Rand does," she panted. "I can't lose him. We mustn't waste precious time!"

"Just exactly what did you see in this vision, Lissa?"

She swallowed past the dryness in her throat. "I saw Abey following Armando's tracks to the church. The Spaniards hid themselves away in a secret room behind the confessional and then—"

"Why don't you just flood the church or burn it down?" he asked. "That would prevent the Spaniards and Rand from going in the place altogether. You can do that, can't you?"

"I've no way of knowing if Armando is already inside and I can't burn it down or flood it if there's even the smallest chance Margaretha is inside it!" Even extending the fog could be just as detrimental to Rand and her sister as it could to Manera and his companions.

"Nay, I guess you can't," said Andries. "But please don't worry so much. Keep in mind Abey is following the tracks of Manera and his friends because he doesn't know where the Spaniards are going. Thanks to your vision, we do. Rand and his men are traveling at a much slower pace, so they can follow those tracks. We aren't. In addition, I would say they had no more than a twenty minute head start, if even that. All of that gives us the time we'll need. We'll arrive at the church ahead of them, I'm sure. Who knows? We may even encounter them before they get there."

"I hope you're right, Andries. I truly hope you're right," she said.

The rustle of trees behind them grabbed their attention. Cornelius yanked his pistol out of his belt and aimed it toward the noise. He cocked the hammer and thrust her behind him.

"Show yourself," he commanded.

With hands raised high a tawny-skinned Spanish soldier, of medium height and build moved out of the shadows.

"Allow me to explain," he said as he shifted his gaze from her to Cornelius and then back again. "My name is Dantae Alexandre. I didn't pursue you as an enemy intent on your capture. Rather, I am here as your ally in the rescue of Margaretha."

Lissa placed a hand on Cornelius's arm. He stared at Dante for several seconds before he lowered his weapon.

"It's all right, Cornelius. I've seen this man before, in a vision. If I'm not mistaken, he and my sister have—at the very least—formed an agreeable friendship. Now please, we have to go."

Dante blew out a sigh as he lowered his arms and nodded. "Our bond goes far beyond friendship, *señorita*. Your sister has my heart and I believe I have hers, as well."

Lissa closed her eyes and sighed.

Despite her impatience, Cornelius eyed the man with suspicion. "Just how long have you been following us?"

"From the beginning of your journey. After the guards took Margaretha from her chamber, I abandoned my post. I knew then I would never return to the fortress. In fact, I left the citadel for the sole purpose of rescuing Margaretha myself. However, once outside, I overheard the conversation between you, your captain and his crew after the ships were destroyed. I decided then I'd follow you, since your captain assigned you to watch over Lissabeth."

"Please!" Lissa cried. "We've got to go!"

"Wait, Lissa," Cornelius said. "Tell me, Alexandre, why would you do that if Margaretha's rescue was uppermost in your mind? What did you think you'd gain? Rand didn't intend for us to rescue Margaretha. Surely you understood that. Wouldn't he have been the better choice?"

"*Sí*, what you say is true. But I hoped I could convince Lissabeth that we desperately needed her help. Trust me, Manera would execute Margaretha on the spot should she become a hindrance rather than an asset. The *padre* would have her killed quicker than that." Dantae turned toward Lissa. "Please, let me come with you. Upon my oath, I will help you deliver your sister from the hands of her captors or die in the trying."

An idea leapt into Lissa's mind. The plan would only work if they arrived at the church well ahead of Rand—

"What do you think, Lissa?" asked Cornelius. "Can we trust him?"

Lissa nodded.

"That's good enough for me," Andries said.

"Now, I beg you, we must hurry or we'll be too late," Lissa said as she gathered the folds of her skirt.

Cornelius waved them forward. "All right then, let's get going. Lissa's right. We're wasting time we cannot afford to."

Macuya led them through the forest with a renewed sense of urgency. All the while, the vision of Rand's death never strayed far from her mind. Those thoughts so occupied her mind that she didn't notice her companions had stopped until she stumbled into Cornelius. As she opened her mouth to apologize, he turned and his finger instantly touched her lips as he steadied her feet. He then cocked his head and gazed pointedly to the left.

Ahead in the distance, was the old, stone church she saw in her vision. From the hilltop upon which they stood, she could only see two sides of the structure. Her gaze darted about in search of Rand or one of his men.

"There isn't any trace of them. I think we must have beaten them here," whispered Cornelius.

"Are you sure?"

"If the scene in your vision had already taken place, we'd see a bevy of Spaniards crawling all over the entire area. Right now they'd be looking for more of Rand's men," he said. "Isn't that right? For now, we'll wait."

Andries nodded. Macuya turned. Did he hear or see something they didn't? He cupped a hand around his mouth and warbled the cry of a bird. The sound of it echoed throughout the forest. Nothing but silence answered his call. Macuya tried again. Then he stooped down and peered through the trees.

Lissa searched the forest as well. She didn't see Rand, or any of his men for that matter. Each minute seemed an eternity for the dread in her heart. What if Rand and his entire crew were already inside the church? What if the Spaniards had already killed them all? Just as she opened her mouth to speak, Abey emerged from the shadows of the woodland. Rand, Wolf, and the crew stepped ahead of the warrior. Yet right now, only Rand mattered. She looked at no one else.

With weapons drawn Rand and his men quietly approached the church. Within seconds he'd be at the door.

No! Lissa bolted toward him. Cornelius and the others were hot on her heels. She wanted to scream out a warning but knew that would alert the Spaniards as well. Instead, she lengthened her stride. Her lungs burned for the effort.

The commotion behind him seized Rand's attention. He whirled toward her. With a look of deadly calm, he lifted his pistol. Lissa squeezed her eyes shut as she flung herself into his arms. At once his arms went around her.

"Lissa," he whispered in alarm. "What are you doing here?"

His eyes blazed with anger as he shifted his gaze toward Cornelius. Before he could berate his bos'n, Lissa placed her hands on his cheeks and turned his face toward her.

"This isn't his fault, Rand," she said. "I'm here against his wishes. He couldn't stop me from coming… not after I had my vision. So he did the next best thing and he came with me. You told them to keep me safe… and that's what they did. I promise you, that's what they did."

Rand eyed her warily. "What vision?"

Lissa released a ragged breath. She shook her head and put her fingers gently against his mouth. "Not here."

Once they were a safe distance away from the

church, Rand asked again.

"A vision that ended with your death, right inside the door of the church. I was so scared, Rand. I thought I might lose you and I just couldn't bear that! I had to come. I just had to—"

A touch of humor replaced his anger. "My impending death yet again? Just who's responsible for these revolting visions anyway? I must have a stern conversation with—"

"Don't, Rand. Don't make light of this, please."

He cuddled her into his chest as an unintentional moan escaped her lips. "Shh, it's all right, my lady. We're all here and safe, isn't that right? You needn't fear."

"I hope not."

He kissed the top of her head. "I gather Manera and his men have taken refuge inside that church. Do I have that right?"

"Yes, they're inside a hidden room. There's a door inside the first confessional booth."

He scrubbed a hand back and forth against his chin as he gazed at the church. "How did I meet my demise this time around, if you don't mind my asking?"

"The tracks led you all to the doorway. But you already know that now. In my vision you walked inside to search, even though the place looked deserted. But the moment you stopped alongside the confessional, someone leaped out of the booth. He had a knife in his hand." She heaved out a breath, closed her eyes, and gulped. "I'll let you use your imagination from there."

"Hmm." He turned his gaze toward the church. "Is that the only way inside this hidden room?"

"I don't know. My vision didn't provide the entire

layout of the church. In fact, because of the darkness, I saw very little. I'm sorry. I can't help you with that."

"The layout doesn't matter, Rand. We could just rush inside and strike the booth," said Wolf. "In fact, we could just topple the thing over before they do any leaping. Manera certainly wouldn't expect that."

"Nay, he wouldn't," Laurens chimed in. "We could have the lot of them surrounded and overpowered before they collect their wits, if they have any, that is."

Dantae's comment about Margaretha being a hindrance instead of an asset bounded to the forefront of her mind. She held up a hand. "I've a better idea. One I believe will work far better for everyone involved and most especially, for my sister. Please remember, her life is still at risk. Will you hear me out?"

Rand narrowed his eyes. "I know you don't think you're going in there. Don't even suggest it, Lissa."

A quiet breath of laughter accompanied the shake of her head. "No, I hadn't planned on doing that. What I can do is lure them out into the open by creating a bit of mayhem. Once they're all milling about the place in search of what they can't find, we'll send Dantae in to fetch my sister. No one will even know we're here."

"Dantae?" asked Rand. "Who's Dantae?"

Lissa turned toward their new companion and beckoned him forward. "This is Dantae Alexandre, the Spanish soldier who happens to be in love with my sister. He caught up with us a short while ago. He vowed he'd rescue her or die trying."

"Did he now?" said Rand with a bit of skepticism to his tone.

"*Sí, Capitan*," Dantae replied. "You need not fear ulterior motives. Upon my life, I will not leave this place without Margaretha at my side."

Rand turned his attention away from the soldier without saying anything at all in return. Instead, he gazed at her. "You think during this confusion you create, Dantae could slip inside the church unnoticed, due to the uniform he wears. Do I have that right?"

"Yes—"

"That might not be as easy as it seems," he said. "In order for that to work without flaw, you must lure every guard out of that room. I don't think Manera would allow all the soldiers to abandon their post, even as foolish as he is. At the very least, I think he would assign one guard to remain with Margaretha at all times, and more likely two."

"That would not be a problem for me, *Capitan*," said Dantae. "I'm confident I can handle the guards, regardless of number. Familiarity with one's comrades has its advantages."

With slow thoroughness, Rand looked the man over. "Perhaps you could at that. However, I think it best to move forward with a bit of caution. Before we put this plan into action, we must consider every problem we might face and then find a solution for it."

Wolf placed a gentle hand on top of her shoulder. "Don't look so worried over the delay, Lissa. Right now, Manera and his men won't go anywhere. I'm sure they think they're safe inside. In all likelihood, they'll stay the night. That gives us time to plan this out in the best of all possible ways, so no one gets hurt."

"More than enough time," Rand replied. "Tell me, Lissa, how did you plan to lure the men out into the open?"

She drew her shoulders together. "Fear."

He did a double take. "Fear?"

Lissa found it obvious he hadn't expected that solution. Neither did the members of his crew. Their astonished expressions almost made her laugh.

Rand shook his head. "Would you explain that a little more in depth, please?"

"Well, Manera is a very superstitious man. So are most of his companions, I'm sure. Because of that, I thought I'd start with some unexplainable noises inside the church."

"Noises? What kind of noises?" asked Wolf.

"With a bit of wind, I could create unintelligible whispers and unexplained knocking against the walls. If you think it'd work better, I could replicate the sound of things being moved about in the chapel itself. With that they'd have to come out and at least investigate, wouldn't they?"

Rand dipped his head and grinned. "Aye, at the very least."

"While they're inside the chapel, I thought I could either conjure the apparition of an angry ghost, or whatever comes to mind, using water, and sand, as well as the wind. With both wind and mist I could also fashion the illusion of large, predatory animals of one kind or another. Don't you think any one of those things would make them come out of hiding?"

"There aren't any large, predatory animals here," Rand pointed out.

Lissa glanced at the church. "Yes, I'm aware of that. All the better though, don't you think?"

"I think she might have something there, Rand," said Wolf.

"Aye, I believe she does." Pieter laughed as he

jabbed Johannes in the ribs. "Such a sight would make a grown man run for cover. So you can just imagine the effect it would have on the likes of Manera, sniveling coward that he is."

"You figured Dantae could then slip inside the hidden room and collect your sister with no one the wiser?" Rand asked.

Lissa bit down on her lip and nodded. "That's the general idea, but you can fill in all of the details I may've missed, can't you?"

He gave her a sideways glance. "What if they believe taking refuge inside the hidden room is a far better option than rushing outside during your mischief-making?"

"Not a wise decision. The visions will simply follow them inside a place they cannot escape from," she replied.

For a time, Rand focused solely on the church. He said nothing as he likely mulled over what she said. His men all did the same. The silence drove her crazy.

"All right," Rand finally said. "I think we'll go ahead and take up positions around every possible entrance and exit before Lissa conjures her misty phantoms. Johannes, I'll need you and Conrad to figure out how many men it will take to cover them."

"Aye, *Kapitein*," said Johannes.

An impish gleam entered Wolf's eyes as he gave Rand a nudge. "You know, I think it might be advantageous in this venture if one of us sneaks inside the confessional while Lissa provides the racket as cover. He could await the first unfortunate victim Manera sends out of his hole to investigate. For surely he would risk no more than one. At least, not right off.

197

The level of anxiety will move up a notch in those remaining when the man doesn't return."

A slight grin blossomed into a full-fledged smile as Rand nodded over the brilliant strategy. "I assume you want the honors?"

Wolf chuckled. "Aye, *Kapitein*. I wouldn't have it any other way."

Chapter Sixteen

Rand spied Wolf as he slipped through the back doorway of the church, carrying an unconscious Spaniard over his shoulder. His first mate dumped the man onto the ground.

"I didn't lift a finger," Wolf whispered, a hint of disgust in his tone. "The man just stepped into the confessional, saw me standing there and passed right out. What kind of a guard does that?"

Joris grinned as he dropped to his knees. With a bit of rope from their supply sack, he bound the soldier's hands behind his back.

"Not the stoutest of heart, but I wager it's all they have. Besides, the fact that he fainted dead away wasn't unexpected by any of us, you know."

"What's that supposed to mean?" asked Wolf.

Joris flashed a grin. "Well, if you ask me, the sight of your face is enough to make anyone pass out."

"You're one to talk, Hoochlandt. Have you taken a good look at your own reflection lately?" he countered. "I'm not even sure your mama could love a face like that."

"All right, let's get serious now," said Rand. "Once they realize their man won't return with his expected report, they'll send more to investigate the cause, I'm sure."

"That, alongside whatever else Lissa dishes up for

their collective enjoyment," said Wolf.

Rand nodded as he looked at Lissa, still deep in concentration. "Indeed, so let's get ready for the forthcoming commotion, shall we?"

While members of his land crew towed the soldier's unconscious body deep into the brush, he and Wolf peered through the dusty, broken window at the side of the church. From this vantage point, they could see the confessional booth without hindrance. The seemingly endless wait set his teeth on edge. As he turned away from the window and toward the hill, Wolf nudged him with his elbow.

"Looks like we've two more," he murmured.

Rand returned his attention to the window. Men skulked about the chapel in search of their missing companion. As they headed toward the front of the church, they stopped dead in their tracks, gaping dumbfounded at the obstacle in their path.

Even the bravest man would cower at the swirling black cloud rising from the floor.

How did she do that with just water, a bit of sand from the shore and wind?

As the apparition took on the form of a monstrous, two-horned demon, the two guards loosed terrified screams. They ran for the door at breakneck speed. Johannes stuck out his boot and tripped them as they crossed over the threshold. They landed face-down on the ground. Members of his land crew hastily bound their hands with rope and toted them away.

"Three down, twelve to go," Wolf murmured. "The rest of them should scurry out of their hole anytime now."

Just as the words left his mouth, a clamor of

footsteps and the rattle of swords sounded in their ears. As the remaining soldiers scrambled through the doorway of the confessional, their resolute expressions changed to horror. Panic ensued. Amidst the terrified screams, several soldiers fired off their muskets. The Spanish soldiers pushed and shoved each other in their haste to get out of the church ahead of their comrades. Still, Manera and Margaretha remained hidden within their sanctuary.

Perhaps Benavides's gutless lackey wouldn't leave it for the fear that assaulted him? The instant the thought crossed his mind, a hand gripped his shoulder. Dantae now stood at his side.

"*Padre* de la Casas," he ground out just as the priest elbowed everyone aside as he raced for the door.

The gutless coward took off running in the direction of the citadel.

"I'll get him," Wolf hollered and took off in pursuit.

In his search for Manera, Rand stayed clear of his crewmen while they apprehended all the soldiers that escaped. Finally, his patience ended. He moved past the uproar toward the chapel door intent on flushing the sniveling, milk-livered scut out of his hiding place. The man would pay dearly for what he'd done.

Manera stumbled over the threshold as he clung to a woman who, with the same shape of eyes and brows, alongside the color of her hair, bore a fair resemblance to Lissa. Dantae bolted forward and yanked Margaretha out of Manera's grasp just as Rand's fist hammered the man's jaw. The fierce blow launched him backward. The boot-licker's eyes rolled back in his head as his body slackened the moment he hit the ground. Rand put a hand on his hip and heaved a disappointed sigh.

Joris smacked him on the back and laughed. "If you had wanted to extract full retribution from the man, then you shouldn't have hit him so hard, *Kapitein*. Still, it's a blow he won't soon forget. Especially since he lost a few teeth for his trouble."

Rand shrugged away the comment as he turned his gaze toward the group of warriors on the hill. With the soldiers captured, and Margaretha safe in the arms of Dantae, Abey bowed his head. Rand returned a casual salute as Abey and his warriors disappeared into the shadows. The Taino had more than repaid any debt they believed they owed. The Spaniards remained ignorant as to their presence on the island.

He gazed at Lissa then. Though he found it obvious she desired a reunion with her sister, she stayed right where she was. He knew then she concentrated on her final task, one he wouldn't let her perform without standing as her guard. Wolf hadn't returned yet. That meant de la Casas could be anywhere. Just as he started up the hill, he encountered Conrad.

Rand aimed a thumb at Armando. "Bind his hands and put him alongside the rest of his companions."

"My pleasure," said Conrad.

His gaze never once wandered away from Lissa as he headed toward her. She smiled as he brushed the wind-blown locks of hair away from her face.

"Are you all right, my lady?"

She nodded. "Yes, I'm fine."

"At a later time, I'll tell you just how very impressed I am with your, uh, exceptional ability to scare the devil out of a bunch of battle-hardened soldiers. But for now, I'm wondering if you'd like some rest before you move the *Draeck* to this side of the island?"

"No, I want it done now so we can leave this place."

"Sounds good to me. Can I hold you while you're thus engaged, or—" He raised a brow while he let the rest of the question hang.

Her smile broadened. "As long as you keep very still and no distractions. Do you hear me?"

"Not a single distraction, I so swear." Rand worked at fighting a grin as he crossed his heart and turned her toward the ocean. He laced his hands about her waist.

Once again, she cradled her talisman and closed her eyes. The heat of her crystal radiated outward. It then grew ever brighter while she embarked upon her final duty. The manifestation didn't take nearly as long as he thought it might. First the vessel appeared as a cloudy haze, hovering just above the water. But as his ship glided eastward, it grew ever more clear and distinct. Lissa turned around.

He glanced at his men, then her. "Shall we finish this mission up and quit the island?"

"Yes, I'm all for that. I'm ready to go home."

Home. They'd yet to discuss what home meant and he hoped that when they did, her definition would match his. However, first they needed a permanent solution to the threat posed by Manera and the *padre*. He would not leave here without the assurance that neither of the men could ever jeopardize his lady or her sister again.

They joined the crew as Dantae talked with the Spanish soldiers. The men were now all free of their bonds, save for Armando Manera. In response to one particular question that Rand didn't understand, Dantae extracted a piece of parchment from his pocket. He handed it to the man who made the inquiry.

Rand turned toward Antonis. "What's going on?"

"No need for alarm. All is well. Just so you know, Dantae commands the utmost respect of these men and he has just exposed Manera and the *padre* for the maggots they are. He laid out in minute detail the plans they concocted concerning Lissa and Margaretha. That one right there just asked Dantae if he had any proof that would support his claims. If so, he said he'd present it to the governor. In turn, Dante said he had intercepted a letter Manera wrote to de la Casa. As you can see, he's reading it now."

The soldier passed the letter to his companions and as they took turns reading it, the Spaniard spoke with Dantae. At the end of their conversation, Dantae nodded and the two men shook hands.

Antonis seemed satisfied as well. "Stefano will escort Manera and the *padre* to the governor of this island, in chains. Apparently, the governor doesn't much care for either of them. Stephano believes with the letter as proof of the forthcoming charges, the governor will see them both hanged."

"Well, Manera, anyway," said Wolf as he stepped into the clearing. "I'm afraid the *padre* has already met his demise. At this moment, he is facing his Maker. Would that I could be a fly on the wall."

Joris placed a hand on his hip as he shook his head. "What happened?"

"The man cared more about the phantom cat that stalked him, than the danger in front of him. He lost his footing and tumbled off the side of a very steep cliff.

'Twasn't a pretty sight."

"Couldn't have happened to a better man, though," said Johannes with an air of nonchalance.

"I'll second that," said Pieter.

"Look, everyone!" Cornelius shouted out as he gazed out over the ocean. "There's the *Draeck*!"

"Excellent," said Laurens. "Let's get a fire started so we can signal Hendrick. He must lower the boats and fetch us with all haste."

Conrad looked over at Lissa and grinned. "Lissa could do it faster than we can."

Rand shook his head. "Lissa's done enough. Take care of it yourself."

Lissa gave him a grateful smile, Then she headed for Margaretha and embraced her sister the instant she arrived at her side.

As she stepped back, she looked her over from head to toe. "Margaretha, are you well? I'm so sorry it took me so long to get here, but—"

"I'm fine. Truly, there's no need for an explanation. Dantae and your *kapitein*'s men have already filled me in on all of the details. I'm both grateful and sorry for all you did and all you endured on my behalf since my capture." Margaretha bit down on her lip. "But please, Lissie, please… You mustn't be angry with me. I didn't know you were coming. I certainly didn't know you were here on the island. And, well… I didn't know what else to do once they took me out of the citadel. I didn't expect any kind of a rescue. So, I believed the only choice I had left was to—"

Lissa's horrified gasp silenced her sister. At once, Rand turned toward Lissa and found her terrified gaze fastened on the ocean's rolling waves.

He looked seaward himself and saw a fleet of misty ships. They sailed straight for the shore at a speed higher than humanly possible. He'd never seen anything like it in all his days at sea. He gathered her into his arms and held on tight. She gulped.

"Oh, Margaretha, what have you done? What have you done?" she whispered.

The sorrow as well as fear in her eyes caged his heart with icy fingers.

"What is it, Lissa? What's wrong?"

A ragged sigh passed through her lips as she closed her eyes. When she opened them again, a single tear cascaded down her cheek. She glanced at the ghostly vessels as she removed her talisman from around her neck and then placed it around his.

"I don't have time. I'll always love you, Rand Van Locken. Always… don't forget. Please, don't ever forget that."

The ships had all but reached the shore. A severe foreboding drove him to wrap his arms around her even tighter. He held her against his chest while a host of ghostly white mists drifted toward them. Her fear had become his fear.

"Lissa, what's going on? Please, you must tell me what all this means!"

She slowly shook her head and touched her lips to his.

Before he could say another word, she and Margaretha disappeared, leaving his arms empty.

Chapter Seventeen

Rand paced back and forth inside Frans Capoen's study. He and the men who had accompanied him ashore caused quite a ruckus upon their arrival here in Sint-Kruis. Most especially after they asked for Lissa and Margaretha.

News of their landing spread like wildfire on withered grass. People filled the streets and looked them over with blatant curiosity. Not that he cared. Everyone they met along the way pointed them toward the governor's mansion. By the time they arrived, numerous locals had gathered outside the iron gates. The man who opened the door after he relentlessly pounded on it, finally allowed him entrance. Just him. Right now, despite Dantae's fervent protests, he wouldn't argue the point.

While his companions cooled their heels outside, the haughty servant who introduced himself as Albert as if he loathed to do so, ushered him inside the study. The man lifted his nose and asked him to wait. The request, which sounded more like a command, annoyed him further. He'd waited long enough. The gut-wrenching crossing from San Juan to this island exhausted what little patience he had left, if he had ever possessed any at all. Every minute of every hour he grieved over and pondered Lissa's sudden disappearance. Dantae didn't have any answers either.

He only had questions.

The hope he held that Lissa would be here, carried him through the most excruciating seventeen-hour voyage he'd ever endured. The fact that no one on this island had seen Lissa or Margaretha since Armando Manera set his plot in motion, harrowed his soul. Rand didn't know what to do or where else to go from here if Lissa's father couldn't give them some kind of direction.

As he waited, he gazed about the opulent room, rich in burgundy and gold colors in both furniture and rugs. A large desk rested against the west wall. It held a stack of parchment and an inkwell and quill. A gold colored sofa with a burgundy floral pattern sat along the north wall. The small round table next to it housed an assortment of refreshments and crystal goblets. To the east of the room, he gazed at a wall-to-wall mahogany bookcase, filled almost to capacity with books. The red brick fireplace was framed with richly carved mahogany side pillars and mantel.

He spun around the moment the door opened. A middle-aged man, dressed in a white linen shirt, dark brown breeches, matching vest and white stockings, entered the room. He was of average height and weight and his golden hair was streaked with gray. His very demeanor bespoke his grief. Nonetheless, his host strode toward him and offered a firm handshake.

"Good evening, sir. My name is Arjaen Capoen. Albert tells me you are Rand Van Locken, *kapitein* of the *Rood Draeck*. He said you have news of my daughters."

His piercing gaze probed deep. Rand expected no less from the man responsible for giving Lissa life. He hoped that by the end of their conversation, the man would find him worthy of his daughter. He swallowed past the knot in his throat.

"In truth, sir, we had hoped to find them both here, safe and sound."

Arjaen swept a hand toward the chairs that faced the fireplace. "Please, have a seat—and I beg you—tell me everything you know about my precious little girls. I need to know why you thought they might be here. No matter how painful, or how absurd, don't leave even the smallest detail out of your report."

He sat down in one of the joined oak and marquetry armchairs, while Arjaen settled into the other. Rand turned his gaze toward the fire and studied the flames. Where to begin? He took in a deep breath and then let it go.

While Rand told his story, Lissa's father didn't interrupt. Rand finally gazed at Arjaen. "After Lissa and Margaretha disappeared, we immediately set sail. All the while I harbored the hope that those ghost ships had escorted them home."

The man's shoulders slumped forward as a trembling hand went to his brow. "I'm sure they did," he said in a quiet voice.

The words confused him. "What do you mean? I thought you said you haven't seen them."

"I haven't. For this island is not really their home, is it?" He paused then cleared his throat. "What you saw off the coast of Puerto Rico is something rarely witnessed. The manifestation tells me that desperation must've overwhelmed Margaretha. I can see that she didn't stop and think about what she asked for. She didn't consider the consequences of petitioning the ghost-*wieven* for help or make clear her desires.

Perhaps she didn't have time before her jailors removed her from the citadel. Either way, it doesn't really matter for the deed is done and can't be recalled."

Rand drew his brows together. "What can't be recalled? I don't understand."

"Nor would I expect you to."

Arjaen rose from his seat and then poured them each a glass of brandy. As Rand accepted the offered goblet, Arjaen downed the contents of his glass in one swallow.

"Other than the spectacle there on the beach, do you know anything at all concerning the ghost-*wieven*?"

"Lissa told me many of her ancestors had chosen to remain behind after their mortality ended. She said they believed they could offer greater service to the living than they could in the world of spirits. Other than that, I don't know anything at all."

"What she told you is true. My wife once told me that many of them are very old spirits. They carry a wisdom no one could possibly attain during their mortality. Therefore, she said, when a mortal stands before the hallowed mounds and petitions their help, the assistance given is not always what is expected or even desired. Yet, it's always best for all concerned if the petitioner would but stop and contemplate the decision the *Wieven* made as well as the help they gave. As a descendant of the *Witte Wieven*, if Margaretha summoned them for rescue and nothing more, then from what you've told me, they heard her plea, even as far away as San Juan. I suspect they then took my daughters unto themselves."

"Unto themselves? Exactly what do you mean by

that remark?"

"I believe the ghost-*wieven* determined that to save my daughters from the life the Spaniards intended they have, they dispatched ships which retrieved them from the citadel in San Juan and then took them into their realm."

Rand bounded to his feet and shook his head as heated anger overtook him. "Nay! I will not accept that. Neither Lissa nor Margaretha *died* on that island, Arjaen. They didn't choose that fate of their own accord, and it certainly isn't what's best for them. They are young. They have lives to live and men to love. What about the children they should bear and watch grow? These ghost-women simply cannot take the fullness of life away from them on a whim. They don't have that right!"

The man tilted his head to the side. "Though certainly not common, the occurrence isn't something that's unheard of in the history of the ghost-*wieven*, I assure you, Rand."

"Well then, if they have power to *take*, whether willing or not, they certainly have the power to *give back* in the same manner."

Arjaen blew out a sorrowful breath as he closed his eyes. "Unfortunately, I don't think that's possible. To my knowledge, once taken, no one has ever returned to the realm of the living."

"Well, it bloody well will happen this time if I have anything to say about it." Rand dropped his hand inside his shirt, withdrew the amulet, and held it up. "This belongs to Lissa. By whatever means I must take, I'll see to it she gets it back. After all, the talisman always finds its way back to the owner, does it not? So tell me, where do I find the home of these ghost-women?"

Arjaen raised a brow. "You'll carry through with this plan despite the odds of success, which I warn you, are miniscule at best?"

"I would fight the very demons of hell to get Lissa back. I'll not live without her at my side. Do you understand that? I love her far too deeply. She is my heart and my soul, and I've not had the chance to tell her that. Now, I'll ask you again, where do I find the realm of the ghost-*wieven*?"

A gleam appeared in Arjaen's eyes as he gazed at the amulet. "Perhaps, if you've room aboard your vessel, it might be better if I showed you?"

"Showed me? Where is this place?" he asked.

"Not far from where I lived in Eefde."

Hope once again took possession of his heart. "I would welcome your help. Besides, I promised Lissa that if you so desired it, I would take you home."

"She thought I might be amiable to that idea, did she?" The promise of a smile turned the corners of his lips.

"Aye, that she did, sir."

Arjaen rose from his chair. "Lissa doesn't miss much. Even as a young child she possessed this gift. She is as perceptive as was her mother, and she's right. I'd like to go home, Rand. I need my family now. I know that I don't belong here. Indeed, I should never have come."

Rand wouldn't argue the point right now. For if Arjaen hadn't, he'd never have met Lissa. "Then we'll leave as soon as you're packed. My men will be at your service and escort you to my ship once you're ready to go."

As Arjaen set about his task, Rand asked Albert to get Dante and Wolf. A few minutes later, Albert bought them into the study.

Wolf gazed about the room before he took a seat. "What in the bloody blazes is going on, Rand? The entire household is in an uproar. Are you responsible for that?"

He waved him off and came straight to the point. "As soon as Lissa's father is packed, we're setting a course for Holland and then taking him home."

Dante rolled his eyes. "Why are we going there? Shouldn't we—"

"Because after I gave Arjaen the details of what happened in Puerto Rico, he believes the ghost-*wieven* whisked Lissa and Margaretha there," he replied.

"And if he's wrong and they didn't?" asked Wolf.

Rand narrowed his eyes. "Then I'll approach these ghost-witches and demand to know where they *did* take them."

"Tell me something, Rand. Are you willing to bear the heartache and disappointment if you don't get the answer you seek?"

"You needn't spend another moment's worry over that. I don't care how long it takes or where I have to go; I'll not leave Dutch soil until I have Lissa at my side."

Wolf's grin broadened. "That's all I needed to hear."

****

For the need of solitude, Lissa wandered into the vast, glorious garden, in the realm of the ghost-*wieven*. She'd never before seen quite anything like this place, not even in her dreams or visions. The very sight took

213

away her breath as did everything else in this sphere. Huge majestic willow trees floated like dancing swans in the sparkling lake before her. From all appearances, they had no root to keep them anchored. Not a single green leaf grew on the overhanging branches either. Rather, the gently flowing fronds grew in dazzling shades of pink, blue, purple, and white. As she gazed upon their unbelievable beauty, some of the trees shuddered as they changed color. Her mouth dropped at the startling sight.

When she arrived, one of her ancient grandmothers told her that every living thing within the realm could think for itself as well as act for itself. So then, did these trees change their colors out of desire? Or did they change in joyous response to the sweet songs of the birds that sheltered in their branches? Not that it mattered, really. For such joy escaped her altogether.

Everything about this realm was beautiful and serene. One could spend a thousand lifetimes in constant awe of its exquisite elegance. Just as easily, one could feel the overwhelming love that existed among the members of this sisterhood. Yet, despite the warm and loving welcome she and Margaretha received, she didn't want any part of this world. Maybe someday in the very far future she might consider it. Just not right now. All she wanted right now was Rand. She wanted his arms around her. And she knew, without any doubt whatsoever, he desperately wanted her in his arms too. She had seen, and even experienced his despair—

"Lissabeth, are you all right, dear?" asked Sytske.

Her great-grandmother many times over, put a comforting arm over her shoulder. The woman was beautiful as was every other woman in this realm. Her long golden hair framed an oval face and sky-blue eyes with finely arched eyebrows. There wasn't a single flaw found in her youthful skin. The gown she wore today shimmered in every color of the rainbow. She led her over to the richly carved bench at the side of the lake and invited her to sit down beside her.

The dear, ethereal soul gazed at her with a great deal of love and concern. The sweet look in her eyes brought all of her tender emotions to the surface. Lissa couldn't speak past the lump in her throat. She buried her face in her hands and sobbed.

"What's this? What's wrong? Are you not happy with us here?"

"Oh, Sytske." She sniffed. "This… this has got to be the most beautiful place ever created, really it is. And, I can't help but love you all. You've all been so very kind. But, the truth is, I didn't ask to be here. Coming here was not my choice."

"Oh, there, there now. Don't be so sad. There's no need. I'm sure in time, when you see and feel the joy in what we do, you'll get used to being here. Indeed, I'm sure you'll come to love it as much as we all do."

"How can I get used to it, when my heart is somewhere else?"

Sytske smiled. "As in your heart is with Captain Rand Van Locken?"

"Yes, it is. He is coming for me, and I want so much—"

"I know he's coming. Believe me. Our hearts do go out to him too. He is a fine man, Lissabeth, with a most noble character. But then, you wouldn't have fallen in love with him otherwise, would you? I am so very sorry for your pain and suffering as well as his, really I am. I wish it could be different." She patted her knee and then rose from the bench. "I may have a solution for you though. Why don't you spend a bit of time in the hall of records? There you'll find innumerable scrolls that exist in our vast library. Each speaks of a time when a dire need was answered by someone within our realm. Countless men, women and children would've suffered terribly, or even died prematurely without our help. You are an extraordinary healer, my dear. I know if you'll just give it a chance, you'll find immense joy here as you use this gift for those who so desperately need it. I'm also sure that, given enough time, Rand Van Locken will become a pleasant, but distant, memory. One you'll always cherish."

Lissa wiped at the tears that cascaded down her cheeks. "No, no, he won't. My love for him is too strong. He is part of me. Can't you understand that? Has it been so long since you were mortal that you don't remember what it felt like to be blissfully in love? To want nothing more than to share your entire life with the man who captured your heart and soul?"

Sytske merely kissed her cheek, smiled and walked away.

Chapter Eighteen

The voyage to Holland took the greater portion of two months. Along the way they battled the ferocity of winds and torrential storms that tested their skill and mettle. Rand welcomed the weather extremes, for they propelled him toward his destination on the wings of his dragon. Somewhere deep in his heart he believed Lissa had conjured the raging wind for his benefit. He didn't speak the thought aloud. For without doubt, most of the men onboard his ship would consider the journey naught but a fool's errand even if they truly understood it.

Throughout the voyage, the entire crew puzzled over his need for solitude. He could see it in their eyes and their carefully worded conversations. As time went on, all but his closest friends avoided him whenever they possibly could. Those that didn't, let him choose the topic and tone, save perhaps Arjaen, Dantae, and Wolf. They didn't steer clear of talk concerning Lissa and Margaretha. What they might find, and what they might not— He appreciated their need to speak of them and for their understanding when he shared his thoughts in return.

When at last they dropped anchor near Amsterdam, Rand called his men on deck before they took to the boats. Their confusion was obvious in their frowns and knitted brows as they gazed at him. They wouldn't be confused for long. With a hand over his heart, he gave each man in turn a nod born of respect and gratitude. They had cheerfully and willingly served at his side, even to the point of risking their lives many times over. He hoped the words he had rehearsed more than a dozen times, would not fail him now.

He cleared his throat and took in a deep breath. "I'm sure you're all anxious to leave the ship. You've earned some well-deserved shore time and I know you'll want to get to it before the morning ends. So, I'll come right to the point. I've made a decision. It's one to which I have given a great deal of thought these past several months. I didn't make the decision lightly or on the spur of the moment. Over the years I've found it one of the greatest pleasures in my life to have served as your *kapitein,* to have earned your friendship, respect, and your trust. Know I will treasure them. Always."

Wolf drew in a sharp breath. The man knew him so well he at once understood what he meant.

Joris didn't fare so well. "Just what are you saying here, Rand?"

"That my life is now headed in a different direction than all of yours, Joris."

Wolf scraped a hand back and forth across his beard. "Are you sure about that, Rand? You know as well as I that it's no light thing to disband a crew. Especially one as well-honed as ours."

Rand dipped his head. "Yes, I'm aware of that. I've discussed this with you before, Wolf. I'll say it again now, and this time in front of the men. The time has come for you to command a ship of your own. I'm confident you'll find a suitable vessel already awaiting purchase in Holland. The skillful shipwrights there are willing and able to make the modification we've discussed at length, especially with Laurens's help." Rand encompassed the entire crew with the sweep of his hand. "Now, should they choose, these great men standing beside you will serve you just as well as they did me. I hope this is their choice. It would please me well for you to all remain together. But if not, I know you can find men just as capable if you look hard enough and are patient in your search."

"Are you telling us you'll never sail again, *Kapitein*?" asked Laurens.

Rand flashed a grin. "Never is a long time, Laurens. So I won't say that. However, I will say I don't have any plans to sail in the near future. At present I have other priorities that are far more important to me. Now, before you all disembark, see Andries about your wages. I made him privy to this decision a while ago. He'll make sure everyone receives an equal share of the gold the *Draeck* now carries. This is my parting gift to you."

Johannes strode toward him then, as did Cornelius, Pieter, Conrad, Antonis, and Hendrick. The rest of his crew followed. Each of them, in their own way, wished him well. He in turn thanked them for their friendship as well as their service.

At the end of the line, he could do naught but chuckle as he gazed at the faces of his men. "No need for the solemn looks. I'm not dying and this isn't goodbye. I expect that in a future day, our paths will cross again and many times over before I meet my maker."

"I hope so, Rand," said Joris. "I truly hope so. I'm

proud to have had you as my *kapitein*. I count it a privilege to have served aboard the *Draeck*."

A chorus of "ayes" filled the deck in response to the sentiment. After a time, his men headed below deck to gather their things and collect the pay they balked at, citing it as overly generous. Nonetheless, they deserved every coin.

Wolf waited until every member of his crew had left the ship before he sought him out. Rand detected a touch of sadness within his gaze.

"Come now, Wolf. One way or another, you knew this day would come. The one thing constant about life, and can always be counted upon, is that it changes."

"Aye, that it does. I'd not hinder your choice nor talk you out of it, even if such were possible." Wolf put a hand on his shoulder and then drew him into a hearty embrace. "I hope you find her Rand and that life brings you all the joy you both deserve."

"I won't stop looking for her until I do. In the meantime, I'll wish for you the same," he replied.

Wolf walked over to the ladder and then stopped. "You'll find a way to let me know how things turn out, won't you?"

Rand returned a casual salute. "You can count on it."

"Good. When you find her, tell Lissa that she means a great deal to each member of this crew, and most especially to me. Tell her I'll never forget her many kindnesses toward me. Also let her know that no matter how long I live, she'll ever hold a special place in my heart."

"I'll see to it she gets your message, but I think she already knows."

****

Before the sun set, he and his two companions had put about five miles between them and the *Draeck*. They were on their way to Arjaen's farmstead in Eefde, which he still owned, and a daughter now rented. The journey would take them at least four days on foot as well as by way of canal.

As the days passed, he grew ever more anxious for the sojourn's end. At times, when they made camp for the night, he could swear he heard Lissa calling to him, urging him not to give up on her. His own desperate desire perhaps, or did she see him coming for her in vision? Mayhap more likely, the months of separation had taken their toll, and he had simply lost his mind.

"Is something wrong, Rand?" asked Arjaen as he passed him a stale biscuit from their dwindling supplies.

"Just my lack of patience," he said.

He pressed his lips together and nodded. "Well, we're almost there if that gives you any comfort. We should arrive in time for dinner."

"And then what?" asked Dantae. "What are we supposed to do once we arrive at our destination? Just how does one go about approaching the ghost-*wieven*, anyway?"

Arjaen shrugged over the question they had all surely considered but never once talked about. "All I can tell you with any certainty is that when one approaches the *Wieven* with a request, they do so with utmost reverence. One should also leave a gift at the foot of the mound. However, when it comes to your particular petition, I've no idea what is proper or expected. No one has ever spoken of it before. At least, not in my presence."

"What kind of a gift?" asked Rand.

"The best of what someone has, from what I've been told. That gift might be some small trinket, a piece of jewelry, rare herbs, or even flowers from a garden. At one time or another, all these things have been offered to the *Wieven*. My wife once told me these women are very well aware of the worth an offering has to the one who gives it and the level of their sincerity. Frivolous requests, or those unkind or evil in nature, are often disregarded. Unless of course, the *Wieven* answers such a request in like manner, much to the detriment of the one who made it."

Dantae nodded. "Do Rand and I make our requests together, or do we approach the ghost-*wieven* by ourselves?"

"Again, I don't know. I would suggest you make your requests individually. Not that it counts for much, but I'll give you one word of advice before you do so. Be very careful how you phrase your petition. Make very sure that what you ask, is exactly what you want, for such is how they'll answer, if they deign to answer you at all. Keep in mind the answer they gave Margaretha."

About two miles shy of the homestead, Arjaen stopped. He turned his gaze in an easterly direction and pointed toward a barely discernable path leading into the darkened forest.

"The hill mound of the ghost-*wieven* is about a mile or so down the pathway. I'll take you after breakfast tomorrow, but it's not all that hard to find. A very large oak tree, far larger and more ancient than all the rest, sits at the base of the mound. For all its twists and turns, it's quite a remarkable sight. The tree has endured all the calamities of nature for many centuries and yet still stands tall and proud."

In less than an hour they were sitting at Arjaen's table with his eldest daughter, her husband, five daughters and one son. Sonja, all but overcome with pleasure and excitement over the unexpected arrival of her father, served them the first hearty meal they'd had in weeks. Rand picked up his fork as he gazed at the chicken, potatoes, carrots, bread and jam. Yet, Rand's thoughts were far from the celebration, conversation and food. Instead, they centered on a hill mound in the forest where he prayed Lissa awaited him. Numerous compositions concerning his request occupied his mind. Each one replaced by the one that followed. He had but one shot to get it right and that unsettled him far more than he'd ever admit aloud.

The daunting task followed him to his borrowed bed where sleep eluded him. Then at last, when he could bear no more of the uncertainty or anguish, he rose from his berth. He crept out of the house without waking a soul.

A canopy of stars and the full golden moon served as his guide as he strode toward the forest, filled with oak, maple, birch and alder trees. The heady smell of damp earth, as well as the calls from nightjars and owls, accompanied his journey. He followed the path until he arrived at the hill Arjaen had described. The huge, twisted old oak tree, eerie in nighttime silhouette, stood as sentinel to the realm of the ghost-*wieven*. One could almost feel the heart and soul of its members within. Did they know he was here? Would they listen to what he had to say?

With a great deal of trepidation, he approached the mound and dropped to his knees. For several minutes he said nothing. The words he had so carefully prepared, somehow escaped him. Yet, right then, he found it didn't matter. He took in a ragged breath. As he gazed up at the moon, the massive tree, and the hill mound, he slowly let it go. Right now he wanted—nay, he needed—Lissa in his arms, forever and always. He'd not wait another second.

"I've been told I must present my most prized possession, leave it at your doorstep, and then plead my cause before you. I've a ship anchored in the harbor near Amsterdam, called the *Rood Draeck*. It is a most worthy vessel and has carried me and my crew on countless voyages. She has been well taken care of, I assure you and is in excellent condition. Of all my possessions, it is the one that means the most to me. I make it my gift to you. Perhaps you can add her to your fleet. In return, all I ask is that you return Lissa to me, in her mortal state, for she is my heart and soul."

Minutes passed, maybe even hours for all he knew. Desperation set in as only unearthly silence met his plea. Even the sounds of nature ceased to exist as he poured out his heart and soul. Why did the ghost-*wieven* ignore him? Didn't they hear him? Or was it because now they had Lissa and Margaretha in their clutches, they just didn't care about his petition?

With nothing left to offer and nothing more he could think to say, he rose to his feet and turned around. His head hung low and his heart was heavy as he followed the long path that would take him back to Arjaen's. All the while grief consumed him even as questions assaulted him.

Did the ghost-*wieven* not answer his plea because they found his gift unworthy? Did they not understand how much that ship meant to him? Did they not know how much he sacrificed and how hard he worked in order to purchase it? How could they not know that there was nothing he valued more on this earth than his vessel? The *Rood Draeck* was his most valuable possession!

Wait. Most valuable possession… Most valuable possession?

At once he whirled around. He raced back toward the tree. Rand's heart thumped wildly in his chest as he approached the ancient mound for the second time. Once again, he dropped to his knees, bowed his head and closed his eyes.

"Please, you must listen. I need you to hear me out… The truth of the matter is, my most valuable possession is the love I have for Lissa Capoen. I wouldn't know how to give you that. For you see, that love lives within me, in my heart, and in every drop of my life's blood. So, I can only offer you a promise. I hereby vow that if you'll just give her back to me alive and well, she'll be treated as the most cherished woman on this earth. For such she is and always will be. Should I ever break that vow, in any degree, then I give you leave to take her back or do with me what you will."

Rand had no idea how long he had lingered on the hill mound. From the position of the stars he knew the dawn would show its faint light in about an hour or so. Still, he'd yet to hear or see anything that indicated the ghost-*wieven* even heard or considered his petition. He shook his head in frustration as he fought his sorrow and despair.

"I refuse to accept this... it can't be too late... it just can't!" he whispered. "You must have a way to give her back to me. I not only need her now, but for every single day of forever."

Not even a gentle breeze stirred the leaves of the tree. An unearthly silence surrounded him. Helpless anger consumed him then.

"Neither Lissa nor Margaretha asked for this. You just took them without bothering to ask what they wanted. You didn't ask if it was their desire to become like you. You've got to know that Dantae is just as devastated without Margaretha, as I am without Lissa. So is their father. You've got to give them back to us. Please... please, I'm begging you. Give Lissa back to me..."

Time dragged on and during those quiet, silent minutes, grief consumed him. Finally then, he accepted defeat. 'Twas obvious now Lissa wouldn't return. Not now, not ever. He closed his eyes against the pain.

"If you won't give her back, then please relieve me of this suffering. I can't live without her..."

No. he wouldn't let it end like this. He couldn't. There must be another way and he vowed there and then to find it. Yet how long would such a quest take? How long would he have to exist without her by his side?

In the very moment he suffered more torment than what he thought he could possibly bear, the sun appeared over the horizon, bringing light to the earth. The warmth and sense of light touched his hands, his face, his eyelids. He rose to his feet. Arjaen would soon wake up and wonder where he went.

But then as he opened his eyes, he discovered the

light and warmth didn't come from the dawn. They came from Lissa's talisman. The illumination of her crystal rivaled that of the brightest star he had ever seen. Rand yanked it off from around his neck. His gaze never left the amulet.

All thought fled his mind as the crystal hummed, softly at first and then louder and more melodious with each passing moment. When it reached its peak, the talisman rose and drifted skyward. The crystal began to spin. Light, in dazzling display exploded all around the hill mound and surrounded him in a burst of stardust. His heart pounded as he stepped back and took it all in. *What the devil was happening*?

"Rand?"

Rand whirled toward the voice, the sweetest voice, in fact, within the whole of the earth. Immense joy, relief, and love tangled themselves all together in one. Lissa, bathed in glorious, ethereal light, stepped out of an open doorway nestled deep in the trunk of the tree, a doorway that didn't exist a moment ago. Her white gown shimmered with diamond dust as she took a single step toward him and then stopped.

The crystal dropped gently into the palm of her hand. Without taking her gaze off him, she placed the chain around her neck and smiled.

Then fear gripped his heart.

The glow surrounding Lissa looked far more otherworldly than it did mortal.

Chapter Nineteen

Rand didn't move. His feet remained rooted to the spot. For the longest time, he just gazed at her. That despair and longing tugged at Lissa's heart. Did he think her a ghost then? She stepped toward him and offered him her hand. If he but touched her, he would know.

He turned his head slightly to the side as he inhaled a shallow breath. "My lady? Is it really you?"

"Yes," she whispered. "It's really me. I promise you, I'm truly here."

Her captain took her at her word. Ignoring her hand altogether, he cuddled her into his arms. He held her so tight she almost couldn't breathe.

"Oh, Lissa... you've come back to me," he murmured before he joined his lips with hers.

The exquisite kiss bespoke the ferocity of the love he had for her, and she returned that powerful love with everything she had inside her. Tears of gratitude and joy spilled down her cheeks for the gift the *Wieven* granted them. Another soul-shattering kiss followed the first, before he'd allow even the smallest space between them. For a while, he did naught but look at her.

Lissa didn't mind. For she wanted nothing more than to drink in the sight of him as well. She had missed him far more than words could possibly express. The overwhelming need to savor this moment in his arms overshadowed all else.

"I love you Lissa, with every whit of my heart and soul," he whispered.

The declaration warmed every fiber of her being. "As I love you and more so than you could possibly know."

He shook his head as he caressed the sides of her face. "I didn't think they'd give you back. At least not without a fight. But just so you know, I wasn't about to give up."

She nodded. "I know. I must admit the possibility of a return seemed remote at best. Yet, I didn't want you to give up on me either. Not ever."

A slight grin emerged. "I wouldn't have."

She sighed as she looked toward the path that had led him here. "Dantae is coming. He'll be here in a few minutes. We must give him his chance to petition the ghost-*wieven* too."

He turned toward the deeper parts of the forest, rather than the path that would take them home. "Care to take a walk with me, then? I haven't any desire to share you with a single soul just yet. Although your father would probably kill me on the spot if he heard that. He's been quite worried."

"I'm sure he is." Lissa gazed up at the diminishing stars. She had no desire to leave the seclusion the forest offered them, either. "He's probably still asleep though. I think you're safe, at least for the time being."

"Either way, I think I'll risk it." Rand tucked her hand into the crook of his arm and strolled toward the thicket. As they walked along he turned to her and raised a brow. "So?"

"So? Are you asking what made my return

possible?" she asked.

"Aye. That would be a good beginning, but I've other questions as well."

She laughed. "It was a variety of things, I suppose. For one, I didn't die. Although I've learned that being mortal isn't a hindrance as far as remaining in the realm of the ghost-*wieven*."

"What's it like? Their realm, I mean."

As countless images flashed through her mind, a smile touched her lips. "The place is at all times filled with this amazing ethereal light. Everything is so very beautiful there, Rand. Mere words are inadequate to describe it. An abundance of serenity, love, and purpose binds these ladies together. I'm told that once there, very few women are of a mind to leave, living or not."

He halted his steps and slipped a gentle arm around her waist. "Did you *want* to stay with them?"

She looped her arms around his neck and shook her head. "No, I didn't. While in the realm of the *Wieven* I had a vision. I saw you as you crossed the ocean. I witnessed your torment and sorrow. I knew them well, for they mirrored mine. That vision haunted me more than any other before because I didn't know the outcome. Then at long last, there you were, right outside the hill mound. I stood just on the other side and waited because I hadn't the power to open the door. You have no idea how much I wanted to walk into your arms. My ancestors understood this. Yet, during the time I spent with them, they didn't give any indication at all that such a possibility even existed. They simply offered me comfort and nothing more. I was so afraid." She shivered.

He cuddled her closer in his arms and rubbed away

the chill. "Well, for whatever their reasons, you don't know how grateful I am they sent you back to me."

"As am I."

She closed her eyes. For a time, Lissa rested her head against his chest and simply gloried in the warmth of his embrace. She recalled her final hour with the ghost-*wieven,* an hour filled with trepidation, anticipation, and finally, exhilarating excitement. She took a half step back.

"You know, the moment the *Wieven* told me of their decision, I couldn't help but believe your profound petition determined the outcome. One of my more ancient grandmothers said she had never heard anything sweeter or more sincere in all of her existence. But, just so you know, these women will hold you to the vow you made."

"Worry not, my lovely lady. For it's a promise I intend to keep all the days of my life, and even beyond that." He dropped to a knee as he cradled both her hands in his. "But I can't very well keep it unless you marry me. You'll do me the honor, will you not?"

Lissa couldn't withhold the joyful tears, nor did she even try. She wiped the first of them away and nodded.

"The sooner the better."

****

With a critical eye, Lissa gazed at her reflection in the mirror. For her wedding day she wanted to look nothing less than perfect for Rand. She wore the shimmering, white gown the ghost-*wieven* gifted her, accented only by her talisman. Blue forget-me-not flowers were woven throughout her intricately braided hair, which flowed down her back.

"Oh, Lissie." Margaretha breathed out as she

looked her over from head to toe. "You look absolutely gorgeous!"

She shifted her gaze toward her now married sister. To make this day especially exceptional, she delayed her own nuptials far longer than what Rand desired. Still, the well-laid plans gave Margaretha and Dantae the opportunity for a special day of their own and a few weeks of wedded bliss. They had just returned from Zetphen, to witness the celebration that would forever unite her to the man she so deeply loved.

From her open bedroom window, a host of boisterous voices descending upon the property reached her ears. Rand's exclamations of delighted surprise gave her the joy she anticipated. A surprise that took a bit of time and conjuring for her to achieve. A smile appeared on her lips. This moment was her special gift to Rand.

She moved to the window and peeked outside as her captain's entire crew gathered all around him. A broad grin appeared on his face as they offered him their congratulations in the way that suited each best. Just as she had asked, Antonis brought along his fiddle.

"You lucky misbegotten rogue," said Wolf as he smacked Rand hard on the back. "I had my doubts she'd accept you if you were fortunate enough to find her, but since we've been invited to a wedding, I guess she did just that!"

Rand chuckled and nodded. "Aye, she did and most willingly I might add."

"Well," said Joris. "That still remains to be seen. She's yet to stand before the preacher, isn't that right?"

Laurens agreed. "Who knows but that she's reconsidered and has fled the house? At this moment, she might very well be heading somewhere far, far away."

"Nay, I can tell you without doubt, she's still inside the house," said Rand. "Believe me, I've been keeping my eye on both exits. I've no intention of allowing my soon-to-be wife the opportunity of escaping me now."

"Ah, but you forget you're dealing with a member of the *Witte Wieven*, Van Locken," said Cornelius. "If you stop her flight, should that be her desire, she may turn you into something so hideous that not even your mother would recognize you."

"Won't happen," Rand said. "You can trust me on that."

He shrugged. "You never know. She just might if given enough time and discovered the proper elements."

Lissa laughed as Johannes, Pieter and Conrad made similar comments. Andries merely grinned over their antics, as did Antonis, Hendrick and Hazael. They needn't worry though. She had no intention of escaping. Not now, not ever.

The friendly insults and camaraderie slowly retreated into a remote corner of her mind as for a time, she gazed at each face that had become so dear to her heart. More than likely, if her visions didn't change course, they wouldn't see many of them again.

Wolf had already purchased his beautiful new ship. In paying her the deepest honor he could bestow, he named the vessel for her sisterhood, despite the raised brows of the shipwrights who didn't understand the significance behind it. Now, every member of Rand's crew belonged to the *Witte Wieven*, save Antonis and Hendrick. Unbeknownst to Rand, the two hadn't given up residence within the *Rood Draeck*. The cousins believed they had a debt to pay and vowed to remain with the captain until they paid their indentures in full. She found it a good thing. Rand couldn't navigate his ship without their help.

"Lissa, are you ready?" Her father stepped into the room.

"Is it time?"

He nodded then put his arms about her shoulders. "Sonja is bossing everyone into their seats as we speak. Yet, before we go, I must tell you how very beautiful you look today. I'm very happy for you both. I couldn't have chosen a better man to walk at your side throughout all the days of your life. I love you girl, always remember that."

"I love you too, Papa," she whispered as he kissed her cheek. "Don't worry about me. Not ever. I believe Rand and I are destined to live a *very* long and happy life together."

She placed her hand upon his arm and turned toward the door. Her father led her out of the house and down a flower-strewn pathway, to her mother's lovely garden. Rand looked so very handsome, dressed in his white shirt, black doublet and breeches. He quite easily took away her breath. The look in his eyes as she approached him bespoke his love and the fiery passion she stirred inside him. She hoped her gaze reflected the same. He winked as she and her father approached the minister.

The man opened his well-worn book. "I've been instructed by the fierce *kapitein* of the *Rood Draeck* to make this short. After all, you listened to the lengthy version naught but a fortnight ago. And, I won't vex the *kapitein* if I can at all help it. Wilt thou, Rand Van Locken—"

"Aye, I'll love and cherish this woman every minute of every hour of forever. Now move on!"

The crowd roared with laughter. The minister simply rolled his eyes heavenward and shook his head.

"And you Lissabeth?" he asked.

Lissa turned toward her beloved captain. "I vow to love and cherish you, Rand Van Locken, every minute of every hour of forever."

The minister smiled broadly as he held his book high above his head. "Then, man and wife! Rand Van Locken, you may kiss your lovely bride."

As Rand kissed her, a deafening roar of whistles and cheers sounded behind them. At once Antonis grabbed his fiddle from off the table, as did her father. As festive music filled the air, Joris grabbed her hand first, just as he did once before. It seemed another lifetime ago.

In the hours that followed she danced with every member of Rand's crew. Each of them spoke of their deep friendship and love they vowed would last a lifetime. She returned the sentiments in kind. Wolf approached her last of all.

He took her into his arms and grinned. "You look lovely."

She dipped her head as she returned his smile. "Thank you, Wolf. Thank you for everything. And most especially, thank you for watching over Rand. I know you could have left his side long ago. Had you done that though, we would never have met."

Wolf chuckled. "Perhaps that is the very reason I stayed."

"Not so. You stayed because you are a good man, with an amazing heart."

"That means a lot, coming from you." He dropped his gaze for a moment as he sighed. "I want you to know that you will ever hold a special place in my heart, Lissa. You and Rand both will. Should it be that our paths never cross again, know that I shall wish for you all the happiness life can bring."

She tilted her head to the side as she regarded him. Should she tell him of her visions? But then if she did, that might alter his course. To save his men, he might do all in his power to avoid the raging tempest he would encounter very soon. However, it was a storm he had to pass through to be as happy with the woman he would come to love, as she and Rand were right now. Wolf deserved such joy.

Wolf drew his brows together. "What is it?"

A breath of laughter accompanied her nod. "Well, it's just that I can promise you one day our paths *will* cross again, even though as time passes, you might think otherwise."

He bowed his head. "That's good enough for me."

"There's one more thing and please don't ever forget it. You'll promise me that, won't you?"

He frowned even as he shrugged. "Aye."

"Should the day come that you believe something so profoundly that you feel that the situation couldn't possibly be doubted, know that you should explore the possibility anyway."

He gave her a sideways glance. "Care to explain that a little more in depth?"

"What? And take away the joy in the discovery?" Lissa halted the dance. She stood on her tiptoes and kissed his cheek. "Just don't forget what I said."

"All right," said Rand as he claimed her hand.

"We'll have none of that."

Without giving Wolf a second glance, he swept her into his arms. Little by little, he led her toward the shadows as they danced.

Moments later they abandoned the festivities in favor of the horses that awaited them. They set a leisurely pace and held hands as they rode side-by-side toward their destination. Then, once they stood outside the door of the small cottage, her beloved husband swept her up into his arms and carried her over the threshold.

Lissa looked over the room as he set her on her feet. A roaring fire blazed in the rustic stone fireplace. A mound of food sat on top of the table in the corner. Her sisters had provided enough smoked ham, bread, jam and sweet-spiced wine to last several days. A bowl of apples, grapes and pears looked delicious and added a bit of fragrance to the room. Fresh flower petals were strewn on top the homespun quilt, which made the bed inviting. All of it, courtesy of her sweet sisters.

Rand approached her from behind and wrapped his arms around her waist. He nuzzled each side of her neck and then turned her around to face him. For a while, he simply gazed at her. Her heart picked up its pace in response to the intensity of his gaze. Surely there wasn't another woman on this earth as deeply loved and cherished as she was.

"I love you Rand Van Locken. There aren't any words that could possibly express how much."

"As I love you, my lady," he huskily replied. "Wolf is right, you know. I am a lucky, misbegotten rogue. In truth, a man like me surely doesn't deserve a woman like you."

"Of all the ridiculous things you could... Just kiss me, Rand."

He cuddled her closer to his chest. Then very slowly and deliberately, he freed her braid of its ribbon and combed his fingers through her tresses. His fingers traveled up and down her spine, which caused a delightful shiver.

"I'm afraid a few kisses, wondrous as they are, will not be enough this time."

Lissa took in a quick breath. Her mouth dropped in feigned surprise. Her hands meandered up his chest. She then laced her arms around his neck as she gazed into his eyes.

"Afraid? I find that most remarkable. Well, my handsome *kapitein,* let me put your mind at ease. You needn't be afraid."

A word from the author…

Making an impossible love quite possible after all…

I am an author of paranormal and fantasy romance. I have (and have always had) a soft spot for fairy tales, the joy of falling in love, making an impossible love possible, and happily ever after endings. I love music, art, beautiful sunrises, sunsets, and thunderstorms.

When I'm not busy conjuring my latest novel, I spend time with the members of my very large and nutty family here in the lovely, arid deserts of southern Nevada. I also pursue my interests in family history, mythology, and history.

~*~

http://www.debbie-peterson.com

~*~

If you enjoyed this story, or any of my work, leaving a review at your favorite book retailer or reader website would be much appreciated.

Thank you!

Thank you for purchasing
this publication of The Wild Rose Press, Inc.

For questions or more information
contact us at
info@thewildrosepress.com.

The Wild Rose Press, Inc.
www.thewildrosepress.com